Write It Right:

Exercises to Unlock the Writer in Everyone

* * *

Workbook #4

Units 7, 8: Scenes; Style/Voice

By
Susan Tuttle

Susan Tuttle

Write It Right:
Exercises to Unlock the Writer In Everyone
Unit 7: Scenes
Unit 8: Style/Voice

Susan's website and blog: www.SusanTuttleWrites.com
Email Susan at: aim2write@yahoo.com
Follow Susan on Twitter: @stuttleauthor, Facebook and LinkedIn

Cover design by: Aaron Kondziela (www.aaronkondziela.com)

A WriterWithin Publication

ISBN-10: 19141465072
ISBN-13: 978-1-941465-07-3

Write It Right:

Exercises to Unlock the Writer in Everyone

Workbook #4:

Scenes, Style/Voice

Dedication

The first unit contained herein, Unit Seven, *Scenes*, is dedicated to my Alma Mater, Daemen College in Amherst, New York. It was there, in the theater department, that I learned the value of drama and the structure of scenes. It is this theatrical training that has helped me bring the visual depth to my work that makes many of my readers feel they are not just reading a book, but are also watching a movie showing on the silver screen in their mind. So, for my Theater teachers and compadres, Sr. Mary Frances Peters (aka The Nun), Rosalind Cramer, Seenie Rothier, Judy Greenman, Toni Smith Wilson, Jackie Gray, Jonathan Wilson, Jim McNeill, Liz Mackay, Darlene Pickering and all my fellow thespians—this is for you. And for Jordan Rosenfeld and Elizabeth George, scene gurus *par excellence*.

Style/Voice, the second unit in this fourth Workbook, and the eighth unit in the **Write It Right** series, is dedicated to my readers, who give me so much encouragement with their insights and expressed enjoyment of my "slightly twisted" mind. You are why I put virtual pen to paper, and let all the people who live in my head see the light of day. Thank you.

Contents

Before You Begin

SUCCESSFUL STORYTELLING LIES IN being able to tell the story you need to tell in the way readers need to hear it. When we do that, we create stories that readers cannot put down. There are many steps along the way. The first three, Character, Setting and Story, are contained in Workbook #1. The next most important element, Point of View, is presented in Workbook #2, and Plot and Dialogue come in Workbook #3. This volume contains the next two essential skills: *Scenes* and *Style/Voice*.

Unlike other books on writing, this volume is designed as a workbook to help you hone your writing skills and find your unique voice. Within these pages, you will find **20 exercises** designed **for writers of all levels.** You will discover the nine major scene types, come to understand the scene question, and learn how to transition smoothly between scenes so that readers remain enthralled with your story. And in the second unit, you will come to understand what constitutes voice and uncover the secrets to your own unique style, a style that will make your stories unforgettable and instantly recognizable as yours and yours alone.

In the few pages that follow is all the front matter that most people simply skip. If you haven't started with any of the other Workbooks, please read what follows, especially the *Foreword* and *The Value of*

Timed Writing. They contain invaluable information you will need to get the most out of these lessons and exercises. Even if you have read it already, please at least skim *The Value of Timed Writing* to reacquaint yourself with the "rules" of each lesson.

And of course, don't skip the book list. They are all treasures for your writing library.

Foreword

WRITING IS MY LIFE. I have a thousand stories knocking on the inside of my head, seeking the freedom of paper. I also love to learn, especially about writing and ways to improve my range and skills. But I'm not very disciplined when it comes to how-to books. If it's not a mystery or suspense novel, I lose interest quickly, even if the subject matter is fascinating.

I found that, for me, the best way to learn something is to teach it to someone else. So, three-plus years ago, I decided to start a group where I could teach what I wanted to learn about writing techniques. If nothing else, it would force me to read those "how to write" books I've been collecting.

I formed the *"What If? Writing Group"* through SLO NightWriters on the Central Coast of California. I began with a group of six writers of various writing skills and genres. We met once a week for two hours to explore in depth a specific aspect of fiction writing. I worried at first that, given the weekly commitment, the group would gradually peter out. But not only did they keep showing up, they started arranging appointments and planning trips around the lessons so they wouldn't miss any!

As the year began winding down, I was sure this group would go on its literary way, and I wondered how to attract a new group of students. But when the year was up only one person left the group, due to health problems. Everyone else wanted to repeat the course. We picked up three new members and started again from the beginning, not sure if the original six students would get anything much from the repetition. To the contrary, we discovered the exercises worked just as well as the first time around—and in some instances, even better. It seems that, no matter where you are in your writing journey, or how many times you do these exercises, they continue to work. Every time.

These writers are now getting published on a regular basis, and winning awards in writing contests. In fact, three of us won first place awards in different categories at the Central Coast Writers Conference in September of 2011. One even came home with three prizes in the competition! For me, this was proof positive that the **Write It Right** exercises had a hand in unlocking the talent of every member of the group. That's why I added an afternoon class and 8 more students.

The writing successes of both of the *"What If? Writing Group"* made me wish I could reach more writers with the materials we'd used. But even if I taught classes all day, every day, I could reach only a limited number of writers—and all of them local. I wanted more than that. I wanted to reach all writers, everywhere.

To that end, I decided to collect all the lessons into a series of 6 little instruction workbooks (12 units in all), a full program called **Write It Right: Exercises to Unlock the Writer in Everyone**. This workbook is the fourth in the series. The first three workbooks (Character, Setting and Story; POV; Plot and Dialogue) are available in print from Amazon.com, and are available as individual units on Kindle.

Introduction to Workbook #4

SCENES ARE THE BUILDING blocks of your story edifice. They cover the framework, or plot, and draw the reader on into the ongoing action. Without viable, interesting and varied scene structure, even the most fascinating story can bog down in the realm of tedium and boredom. Knowing the ten styles of scenes and the nine different scene structures and when to use them; understanding, crafting and answering the scene question for each scene; and being able to transition smoothly from scene to scene without bogging down in too much exposition will lift your stories from the ordinary to the extraordinary.

Think of the greats of literature: Shakespeare, Dickens, Conan Doyle, Hemingway, James Clavell, Stephen King, Elizabeth George, Sue Henry, Isak Dinesen, Tess Gerritson, J.D. Robb, Janet Evanovich, Kathy Reichs, Anne Rice, Roger Zelazny, Isaac Asimov, Patricia Cornwell... Each has a distinctive style all their own. You know who wrote each novel simply by the way the words are put together, the way the story is structured, the level of vocabulary and the choice of words used in each scene. A confident, unique style/voice brings the story alive for the reader. Therefore, each writer must develop his/her own voice and style, one readers can connect with and recognize even if the author's name is missing from whatever they are reading. The more unique a writer's voice and style, the more that writer will be remembered by readers. And the more his/her work will be in demand.

That is where this Workbook comes in. The eleven exercises in Unit #7 will give you the strategies you need to understand scene and scene structure and how the different types of scenes work in the telling of a story. There are nine exercises in Unit #8 that will help you discover your own personal voice and style and become confident in your uniqueness, so that your stories truly become an extension of your creative self.

It won't happen overnight. It takes practice. But the more you work with Scenes and Style/Voice, the more easily you will be able to incorporate these skills into your narratives.

It doesn't matter what level you are: beginner, intermediate or advanced. These exercises cross those boundaries and address where you are now in your writing career—and get you to where you want to be.

These are not time-intensive sessions. You only need to **dedicate approximately 30-45 minutes** to most of the twenty activities (a few may take longer). Feel free to move at your own pace—one or two exercises a week or a month—but if you choose a fast-track pace, do give yourself enough time assimilate each lesson. It's best to have a couple of days between each exercise. (The *"What If? Writing Group,"* which has used these lessons for over three years as of this writing, does one or two exercises per session, with a week between sessions.)

All you need is a timer and something to write with—pen and paper or computer and keyboard, whichever is most comfortable for you. For maximum results, you might want to pick up a copy of some of the books I've used to formulate these lessons, and which I will reference throughout the course. It's not necessary, though it does make understanding some of the concepts easier.

You can use this volume as a workbook, filling in the pages (though you will need extra paper to finish most of the exercises) as you work through the lessons. But it is best to use separate sheets of paper, or work digitally in a word processing program, so that when you return to the lessons as you feel the need you won't be distracted by previous answers to the lesson questions.

Always remember, **this is an ongoing process**. Writing is a dynamic art and life is a journey through which you are always growing and learning. Over time your writing will expand and deepen to reflect these life experiences. When you finish this volume (or any of the exercises in the other volumes), you can repeat each of the exercises again, just as we do in "The *What If?* Writing Group"—which at this writing is just beginning its fourth year of repetition, with the same students. You'll find that the second, and even third, time around your writing will reach even deeper layers and take you to greater heights. It will be stronger, more compelling and more exciting.

It's a fantastic journey. Plunge into the exercises in *Write It Right Workbook #4: Scenes and Voice/Style* and experience what it means to really understand the narrative potentials available to you.

The Value of Timed Writing

MOST OF THE EXERCISES in this course are timed. You have a specified amount of time to complete each one, usually 15 or 20 minutes. Thirty at the most. That's it. Period.

Why timed writing? There are two major benefits to timed-limited sessions. As **Natalie Goldman** shows in **Writing Down The Bones**, timed writing exercises force you to keep writing. You have a specific goal and only a short time in which to accomplish it. You have to step out of your way, turn off your inner editor—who is constantly telling you you've used the wrong word, no one will believe that plot, your characters aren't "real" enough, etc.—and simply write. From your heart, from your subconscious instincts, from the place where your stories live. It's authentic writing that's scraped to the bone of emotion. It's compelling and readers will want more.

The second benefit is that you learn to trust yourself and your writing process. When we learn to put our conscious mind on hold and just let the words flow, amazing things happen. Stories emerge that we never knew were there. Connections get made that our conscious minds would never have considered. Best of all, our authentic voice emerges, announcing in clear, ringing tones, "This is who I am as a writer. This is what I need to say." Timed writing exercises will introduce you to yourself.

Timed exercises allow you to step away from your editor self and into your writer self because you don't have time to think. You have to just keep writing, no matter what comes out. It may be hard at first not to go back and correct that word, rethink that action, direct the flow, etc. It takes time to learn to trust your instincts. When you find yourself wanting to go back, don't. *Write* about wanting to go back until you return to the natural flow of the exercise. You can always cut out the extraneous parts later. That's what editing is for.

Timed Writing Format "Rules"

Read the lesson, make sure you understand what to do, then set your timer and write until it dings. Don't stop to think, don't edit as you go, just keep your pen moving or your fingers typing on the keyboard. If you can't think of anything at first, write about not being able to think of anything and just see what happens. Repeat for the next lesson. And the next, and the next...

Also, be aware that my use of the terms "character," "person," "people," "he" and "she" are meant to indicate the protagonists, antagonists and other characters in your stories, whether they be humans, animals or otherworldly creatures. Make whatever adjustments you need to make to each exercise, so that it fits your specific genre and character choice.

Note: An asterisk at the end of an exercise denotes that there is an example of that exercise from my own writing at the end of the section.

Recommended Book List

THESE BOOKS, AMONG OTHERS, have been instrumental in the formation of these lessons. Throughout the course I will reference the pertinent page or pages to read in the appropriate volume. Although you don't need these books to complete the lessons, the information they contain is invaluable. It will add to your knowledge and skills and enhance your learning throughout this series. And they will form a solid foundation for your writer's reference library.

I am listing the copyright year for each volume, so that if you want to read the suggested pages, you will have the correct volume in which to find them. How-to books are often updated with new examples and insights. If you obtain a volume published after the dates listed below, you will still get the same fantastic writing information. But because things will have shifted around in newer editions, you might have trouble finding the proper references for each lesson unless you use a volume with the same publication date as those listed on the next page.

Write Away by Elizabeth George (2004)

What If? Writing Exercise for Writers by Anne Bernays and Pamela Painter (1990)

On Writing by Stephen King (2000)

Characters & Viewpoint by Orson Scott Card (1988)

How to Write a Damn Good Novel by James N. Frey (1987)

The Novel Writer's Toolkit by Bob Mayer (2003)

Finding Your Writer's Voice: A Guide to Creative Fiction by Thaisa Frank and Dorothy Wall (1994)

The 38 Most Common Fiction Writing Mistakes by Jack M. Bickham (1992)

Make A Scene: Crafting a Powerful Story One Scene at a Time by Jordan E. Rosenfeld (2008)

And every writer's library should contain the following reference volumes:

***The biggest dictionary** you can afford (check used bookstores for bargains). There's no substitute for a good, print dictionary

Roget's Thesaurus

Sisson's Synonms (if you can find it)

The Elements of Style (Strunk and White)

Barron's Essentials of English

Unit 7: Scenes

Before you begin to write a sentence, imagine the scene you want to paint with your words. Imagine that you are the character and feel what the character feels. Smell what the character smells, and hear with that character's ears. For an instant, before you begin to write, see and feel what you want the reader to see and feel.

~Othello Bach

SCENES ARE THE BUILDING blocks of your stories. Like the stone and wood that create the face of an actual building, or the muscle and skin that cover a human skeleton, scenes are the flesh of your story. They form the shapes, the contours, the attractive facade of the events that occur. Scenes hold the whole together, draw in readers, and don't let them go.

As Jordan Rosenfeld writes in *Make A Scene: Crafting a Powerful Story One Scene at a Time*, "Scenes are capsules in which compelling characters undertake significant actions in a vivid and memorable way that allows the events to feel as though they are happening in real time." It's easy to understand that action is a major, and necessary, component in all scenes, since the characters must undertake some kind of action for the story to move forward. But is action all there is to a scene?

Consider this: Scene 1 is filled only with hard-hitting action, followed by action-filled scene 2 and action scene 3 and action scene 4. Nothing but action; hard, driving and unremitting. After a while, readers will become sated on action and it will no longer have the same power over them as in the opening scenes. Too much continuous hard-driving action only creates anxiety. Readers will need to put the story down just to have time to breathe. And who knows if they will pick it up again, since only more of the same is in store?

So, obviously, you have to use different types of scenes, with differing kinds of action and pacing, in order to continue intriguing readers until the last page. But what are the different kinds of scenes? How are they structured? When does a writer use each one in the story? How does one achieve the proper balance among the various scenes in a story? And most importantly, what needs to be in each and every scene, no matter what kind it is?

The purpose of each scene in your tale is to advance the story, to move it along to its inevitable conclusion. Any scene that does not accomplish this has no place in your tale. Additionally, there must be a clear point of view for the scene as it unfolds. Complex, multi-layered characters who are in the process of growth and change must engage in meaningful dialogue that has its own agenda (see **Workbook #3: Plot, Dialogue** for a lessons and exercises on crafting effective, realistic dialogue). Conflict and drama must test the characters and reveal their personalities, and it must all be wrapped in a rich, enticing setting that pulls readers into a world that feels real. Also, each scene must give readers the impression it is happening right now, as they are reading, even if it is stated in past tense. Unless used as their own type of scene or for short transitions between scenes, pure narrative summary and exposition have little place within the majority of the scenes you will write (see *Lessons #7, 8 and 9* for more on narrative and its variations). Nothing kills an action scene faster than lading it with an overabundance of narrative summary or exposition.

For clarity, here's an example, of the beginning of a scene from about halfway into my story, "Coffin of Silence," with notations on the parts of a scene in brackets:

Far from civilization, the car bounced **(past tense)** down an overgrown dirt track. She **(third person POV)** parked deep in the shadow of an ancient oak and studied the long-abandoned farm buildings. Stars glimmered through gaps in siding and roofs. Ghosts flitting in the dark shadows were the only moving things in sight. **(Physical setting that evokes an eerie atmosphere)** A rusty old station wagon stood a dozen feet away. So he's here, she thought. Let's get this over with. She checked her purse and got out of the car. She scanned the darkness around her, then slung the chain strap onto her shoulder and walked toward the chicken run crumbling between house and barn.

He was there, cigarette end glowing red in the darkness like a manic evil eye. Twenty feet separated them when she stopped, her mouth suddenly dry. They stared at each other in silence.

Finally, without taking his eyes off hers, he dropped the cigarette, ground it beneath a booted toe and stepped closer. **(Action that provides a sense of real time)**

"Well, well, well." He sneered. "Just look at you. Robin Sidowski." **(Dialogue)** His gaze dropped down her lean, wiry body, then returned to the hands that held the purse clutched to her stomach. "Oh. Excuse me. I should have said Robin Berlys, shouldn't I? Mrs. Donald Berlys. God, what a crock."

The contempt in his tone stabbed into her. He was spoiling for a fight. This wasn't going to be easy. She'd forgotten how intimidating his solid six feet could be. **(Physical description to evoke character)** But she didn't rise to his bait. She merely glanced down at the wedding ring sparkling in soft moonglow and returned her gaze to his.

"Did you bring it?" he asked.

"Did you?"

"It's here," he replied, pulling a large Manila envelope from beneath his windbreaker. "Not that it matters, most of this is public record. Anyone has access to it." **(Dramatic tension and plot information)**

"But only you would know to look," she said, unable to keep the bitterness from her tone.

He cocked an eyebrow. She stepped forward, lips parted, right hand stretching for the envelope. He lifted it above his head, just out of her reach.

"Uh-uh. The money first."

"And when you get it, you'll go away and never come back again, right?"

His sharp gaze raked her body once again, catching on her breasts, on silk-covered nipples peaked from the chill air.

"Maybe." His voice was so low she could barely hear it. "I think I'm changing my mind." **(Dramatic tension ramping up and more plot information)**

"What the hell does that mean?"

"It means I'd start saving my money, if I were you."

His thin lips stretched in a ghoulish smile. Moonlight painted his pale hair silver, turned the down on her arms, never very dark and lighter now, to glistening white. **(More detailed description to evoke character and drop clues)** Robin turned her head and bit her lip. She had never hated him more than she did right now.

There is, obviously, more to this scene, but from the opening of it you can get the idea of how all the elements add together to produce a result far beyond the mere sum of its parts.

Each scene, just like the story itself, must also contain a question—a scene question that will pull the reader through in an effort to find the answer. If writers don't know the scene question to each of the scenes in the story, they can wander far from the main plotline and end up with ineffective scenes that may be well written but that don't serve the story. And that puzzle readers and make them put the book down.

So, to summarize, each scene must include complex characters in the midst of growth or change interacting through concise dialogue that advances the plot and provides information, as they deal with rising tension and conflict in a way that feels as though it is unfolding in real time, unencumbered by narrative summary or exposition.

In a nutshell, **each Scene must:**

1. **Include complex characters in the midst of change or growth;**
2. **Have a clear point of view;**
3. **Unfold as though in real time;**
4. **Contain rich dialogue when appropriate;**
5. **Impart new information that advances the plot and deepens characters;**
6. **Use conflict and drama to test characters;**
7. **Evoke a rich setting that allows readers to see and enter the world you have created;**
8. **Contain a spare amount of narrative summary or exposition;**
9. **Pose and adequately answer the scene question.**

Sounds fairly easy, doesn't it? But, like Point of View (POV) and Plot (see Workbooks #2 and #3), it's easier to understand intellectually than to put into practice. Here in this workbook you will find 11 exercises that will help you assimilate the essentials of scene creation into your storytelling genes, so that all your stories will entrance your readers as they live the story along with your fascinating, complex, compelling characters.

I am using scene structures as identified by Elizabeth George, because it is easy to understand how they are put together. They give concrete methodology for each type of scene. Other writers identify scenes in different ways, but I have found the scene terminology I use here to be the most flexible and also the most easily understood.

Jordan Rosenfeld, in her wonderful book *Make A Scene*, delineates scenes according to type (what is accomplished) rather than structure (how the scene is constructed). The scene types she discusses can fit into any of the scene structures you will be working with in these lessons. She identifies **ten scene types**; Opening, Suspense, Dramatic, Contemplative, Dialogue, Action, Flashback, Epiphany, Climactic and Final. Any one of these scene types can be structured according to the scene structures in the following lessons. In other words, a dialogue scene can have a Present-Past-Present structure, a Sight vs. Sound structure, or a Mind to Action structure, etc. So can a contemplative scene, or an action scene or an epiphany scene, and so on. For a thorough review of these scene types, pick up a copy of *Make A Scene*. Every writer should have a well-thumbed copy in their personal library. Jordan's insights are invaluable.

Also, for this unit I will give examples of each type of scene structure as part of the lesson, instead of putting the examples at the end of the unit, as I have done with the previous six units. This is because I think that an example, along with the description of the structure, will give you a clearer picture of how the structure works in an actual scene.

So get out your pen and paper, or fire up your computer, and get ready to delve into scene structure.

Unit 7, Scenes: Contents

Lesson #1: The Motion Picture Scene

IMAGINE THE OPENING SHOT of a movie about the lives of three high rollers in Atlantic City, New Jersey. It starts with an eagle's eye view of the Atlantic coast of America, slowly zeroing in on the area below New York City—the Jersey shore. The camera pans in closer and closer. Topographical elements come into view; hills, roads, trees, lakes, rivers. Cities and towns begin to appear. We spiral down even further and there are the beaches, the towers, the piers and boardwalk of Atlantic City. Closer and closer we come, until one specific casino fills the screen. And the camera brings us through the front door into the main casino room where gaming tables and throngs of people fill the space. We move in past the blackjack tables, the craps tables, the slot machines and stop at the roulette wheel, where three buddies have racked up a small fortune. Then the camera locks onto one face in particular as the actor prepares to lay a bet. Someone grabs his arm and the action begins.

A great many movie and TV shows begin this way, with a Motion Picture Scene. They begin out at a distance to establish where the story is to take place, then move down to the characters who will figure in the scene, then the action starts. In the film industry, this is called an "establishing shot," since it orients the viewer to where the action is taking place. You see it used pretty much in TV shows every time the program comes back on after a commercial break. The waterfront, boats and police buildings in Miami (CSI: Miami); the beaches, surfing and hula dancers on Oahu (Hawaii 5-O); the casinos, police buildings and lab in Vegas (CSI); after the break, all these reorient the viewer as to where the story is continuing to take place. In writing, the Motion Picture Scene quickly establishes the setting for the reader, which can be vital if the reader has been taken away from this particular area for a chapter or two.

A Motion Picture Scene might not be appropriate for a short story that has only one setting, but if it's a long story with a few different settings to complicate things it might be just what you need. And in a novel, there are many places where the reader's attention has been distracted by a new character, a new setting or a new action, and needs to be re-directed when returning to an ongoing plot point. This is especially true if you employ an alternating point of view, in which the story alternates between two or more characters with a variety of settings.

For instance, you are writing a story about three sisters, Grace, Sally and Norma, who live in separate parts of the country. Grace lives in New York City, Sally in a small midwest town and Norma on an isolated farm in Oregon. Using the Motion Picture technique to show an eagle's eye view of the farmland surrounding an old log cabin farmhouse will let the reader know we are now to read about Norma's life. When the next scene shows a city skyline from above, and then zeroes in on high rise apartment buildings and then one specific apartment, we will immediately understand we are now with Grace in New York City.

So, for the Motion Picture Scene, you will begin with the camera out at a distance to establish (describe) the setting, then move closer to delineate (describe) the characters, then move in close as the dialogue and action begin.

It will look something like this, a scene in the second volume of my YA Unification series, a novel in progress (with scene elements noted in brackets):

> The valley looked dead from the hilltop. Trees, bare of leaves, stretched skeletal fingers into the lavender sky as though to scrape away the sickly yellowish-gray clouds. Tassel-topped reeds lay limp along the ground, too weary to raise their heads. Shrubs baked to an indeterminate hue of ennui melted toward the cement-hard clay beneath their feet. A small lake lay inert in the center of the vast bowl, its still surface looking more like tarnished mercury than water. Nothing stirred, neither bird in the sky nor animal on the dun-colored ground.

(Establishing the setting)

> In the far distance, a mirage shimmered, seemed to waft closer to the lake. A white ribbon shot through the scintillating dark column, and slowly resolved into three wavering forms—two large, black shapes bracketing a bright, smaller figure. Menja Solon sat in his saddle on the hilltop, eyes narrowed until he was able to recognize the three: Ardri and Zenon, the Regent's personal guard, with Meleia captive between them. **(Delineating the characters)**

> Sweet Melia. He'd give up his life for her, to keep her safe. Which was about to happen, he thought as he spurred his horse down the ridge, through wilted reeds that crackled with his passage. He'd always known this day would come, that he was destined for great

things. It didn't matter that most would call it treason. Menja knew it for what it truly was—liberation. The restoration of his house to the land. That was worth a life, even his.

"Hold!" he called out when he reached to valley floor. "You are trespassing on Kador Solon's Land. And I believe you have something I want for myself." **(Dialogue and action begins)**

The Regent's Guard drew swords and wheeled to face him. Meleia raised her head and stared at him with wide eyes. Her hands, bound at the wrists to the saddle's pommel, bent her over her horse's mane.

"You dare accost the Regent's Guard?" one of the mounted warriors growled.

"Oh, aye," Menja said. He drew his own sword, smiled his avarice and saw Melia cringe. "As I said, you have something I want. I've come to relieve you of it."

As you can see, once the action starts the short narrative and/or exposition at the beginning of the scene ends. It is used merely as a device to orient the reader as to place and characters, then is dropped as the action commences.

READ: *Write Away* (George, 2004) pages 143-144.

Exercise #1: The Motion Picture Scene

(Purpose of Exercise: to explore the motion picture scene technique)

WRITE A SCENE BETWEEN two or more people that uses the Motion Picture Format. Start out at a distance to establish the scene/setting, then move in to describe the characters, then start the action and/or dialogue. Concentrate on enticing the reader to continue reading through your narrative description and, if possible, by dropping clues to the coming action.

Make sure you **do not overdo** the narrative beginning of the scene. The point is to orient and entice the reader as economically as possible, to establish mood, and to get to the action as quickly as you can while still painting a full picture of the setting and characters involved.

Set your timer for **15 MINUTES** and begin by crafting a bird's eye view of your setting, then move closer to the characters and then dive into the action. Start now.

Lesson #2: The Sound vs. Sight Scene

THIS NEXT TECHNIQUE STARTS with more of a bang than the Motion Picture Scene. It jumps directly into dialogue **before** stopping to address the setting. It sets the pace for the action and lets the reader know which character or characters will be involved in the scene. The writer then backs off and discloses the setting. Then the scene moves back into the dialogue and action.

This type of scene is faster paced than the Motion Picture Scene, and involves the reader much more quickly. The key is to make sure the opening dialogue catches the reader's attention, so that it will draw the reader through the description of the setting and back into the continuing action.

Choose the setting details judiciously for this scene technique. Boring or overly intricate details will turn readers off. Try to concentrate on those details that enhance the ongoing action, that reveal character or that drop clues to future events.

Here's what a Sight vs. Sound Scene looks like, from my paranormal mystery in progress, tentatively titled *Tattooed In Death*.

"Where's Detective Dimwit?" Mackenzie laid her hands flat on the Formica counter. "I need to see him. Now." **(Dialogue—"sound"—opening)**

The station looked the same as the last time she'd been there. **("Sight"—setting description—portion of scene)** But since this time she'd come in on her own and not dragged through reception into interrogation, she had more time to appreciate its luxurious appointments. The room stretched across the front of the building, perhaps thirty feet, but was only about fifteen feet in depth. A narrow wooden bench sat alongside the front door, an iron bar fixed to the wall where a person's shoulders would be when sitting. Probably where handcuffs were affixed while criminals awaited processing, Mackenzie thought. The stained wood was pitted, splintering in places as though sharp pieces had been pried off to use as lockpicks.

The room's only exterior window, narrow and barred, sat to the left of the glass entrance door. The walls sported a peeling coat of industrial green paint. Where it had flaked off a lighter green showed through, giving the place the look of leprosy. Sad, yellowing posters of wanted criminals lined the side walls, half of the faces decorated with vampire fangs, VanDyke beards and demon horns. The reception counter stood in the center of the long interior wall that framed a glass-block window with a miniature cut-out behind which a uniformed officer sat. To the right of the window stood the sturdy locked metal door that gave access to the inner workings of the station.

"Who?" the officer behind the window asked. **(Return   to "sound" portion of scene)**

"Dimwit." Mackenzie kept her voice calm and precise, though what she really wanted was to scream like a banshee. "Detective? Tall, overweight, overbearing and arrogant? In charge of The Tattoo Killer case?"

She raised her brows at the final question and the officer blinked. Recognition finally filled his eyes.

"Oh. Detective Dunwitty. No, sorry, he's not here."

"Really?" Mackenzie narrowed her eyes and leaned forward, stuck her head against the three-foot-square opening. The officer, who looked about thirteen years old—rookies, Mackenzie thought with exquisite disdain—leaned back in his seat. His hand hovered over a panel studded with buttons, some lit, some not.

"Yes, ma'am. I mean, no, ma'am. Detective Dunwitty's not in yet."

"Are you sure? Absolutely sure? He's not hiding in the back, afraid to face me, is he? You want to check on that, little boy?"

"Ma'am, please." The child in the patrol uniform pulled himself up in the seat. "If you can't control yourself I'll have to ask you to leave."

"Leave?" Mackenzie smiled her wrath and again the officer shrank back in his seat. "And here you were so anxious I stay for 25 to life just last week. Where the hell is he?"

A pair of hard arms slid around her from behind. Two huge hands placed themselves on the counter on either side of hers.

Mackenzie could feel the heat radiating off the body behind her as she turned around, her heart hammering in her chest, knowing it was him. The detective who was making her life hell.

"Stop terrorizing the help, Ms. Straite," he growled, his face mere inches from hers. She could smell his lemony aftershave and the salami he'd eaten for lunch. "And the name's Dunwitty, not Dimwit."

Mackenzie stared straight into his deep black eyes and suppressed a shudder.

"Really?" She smiled at him and batted her lashes. "You could have fooled me."

You can see that the dialogue starts with urgency. But the reader doesn't know where Mackenzie is until the description of the setting begins. I use the description of the station to underscore the seriousness of the situation in which Mackenzie finds herself, and to serve as a reflection of the underbelly of life that is now surrounding and threatening her. Then the dialogue and action begins again, drawing the reader even further into the scene.

READ: Write Away (George, 2004) page 144-145.

Exercise #2: The Sound vs. Sight Scene

(Purpose of Exercise: To explore the sound vs. sight technique)

WRITE A SCENE BETWEEN two or more people that uses the Sound Versus Sight format; i.e., start with dialogue, then move out to describe the setting, then go back to the dialogue. You can rewrite the previous scene if you want, starting with the same dialogue and forming the scene into a Sound Versus Sight format. Or you can write a completely new scene for this exercise.

If you are working on a novel or a long short story, you might want to play with various scenes from that story as you go through these nine exercises. Or you can create one scene that you render in all nine of the variations. Or simply write whatever comes to mind when the exercise starts. The important thing is to concentrate on the specific technique in each exercise.

Give yourself **15 MINUTES** to complete this exercise, rendering the Sight vs. Sound scene technique. Start writing now.

Lesson #3: The Present-Past-Present Scene

ELIZABETH GEORGE CALLS THIS technique the Present-Past-Present Scene. In a nutshell, it encapsulates a short flashback within a present-action scene.

This is a great technique to use when the reader needs to understand something that happened in the past that has not yet been revealed, and that also has great influence on what is happening in the present. To create a Present-Past-Present Scene, you begin with a scene in real time, then partway through it you back away and insert a flashback mini-scene that reveals the impetus for the present action, then return to the present-time scene until it is finished.

It is important to remember that you cannot stick just any flashback situation into this scene technique. What is flashed back to has to be **the action that drives the present action forward.** This is not the place to reveal that Uncle Joe borrowed his older brother's cufflinks and lost them just because it's an interesting factoid in Uncle Joe's biography that tickled your fancy when you thought of it. But, if the fact that Uncle

Joe lost the cufflinks leads to the detective solving the mystery, then that makes it a prime candidate for the "past" part of a Present-Past-Present Scene.

Here's an example I wrote in one of my classes of how the Present-Past-Present Scene technique works, with the Present-Past-Present parts noted for clarity.

Carlos burst through the door and raced onto the roof. **(beginning of Present part)** Heat seared his bare soles. The gravelly texture of the asphalt surface abraded his heels as he skidded to a stop and looked around. They were close behind him, he knew, his so-called friends. As if anyone could be a friend to someone like him.

The heat was becoming intolerable now. He hop-skipped over to the roof's edge and peered down. His head dizzied at the sight of the nine story drop and he almost lost his nerve. Then a ringing echoed in the air, feet slamming on metal stairs, and his back stiffened. His resolve solidified. He glanced behind him at the open doorway, then set his hands on the waist-high parapet.

It was harder than he'd thought it would be to hoist himself onto the narrow ledge. He scraped his shins on the stone and they began to bleed, to sting, little needles jabbing into the pit of his stomach. His muscles twitched. His knees felt unhinged when he pushed himself upright.

It was as though his strength had been siphoned off somehow. Carlos thought of Rachel, of the night he gave in to himself, the night that never should have been, and thought maybe that's what had happened. Rachel had looked like an angel when she'd arrived at his place, not a demon. **(beginning of Past part)** He'd opened the door with unsteady hands and a stuttering heart, not sure what she wanted with him. But he was willing to let her in, to listen, because she'd said the magic word on the phone: Shelby.

Rachel made them drinks and they chatted, inane conversation that had ramped up his anxiety level until he had trouble breathing. Then Rachel set down her empty martini glass and smiled at him.

"She's waiting for you, Carlos." Her voice was so low he had to lean close to hear.

"Shelby?" His disbelief rang in his tone, in the silence of the apartment. "Impossible. She's gone. Wants nothing to do with me, not after what she found out."

Rachel smiled.

"All of them are waiting for you. Will you come?"

"It's not right." He shook his head. "I'm not who you think I am."

"Then who are you? What are you?"

The room tilted. Rachel receded, then her hand snaked out and lifted the cocktail glass from his fingers. Starbursts of glorious color streamed from his eyes, limning the room in fairy dust. He lifted his hand—it seemed to take hours—and looked at the nine fingers that flexed from his palm. The drink, he thought.

"What did you—" he asked, but his mind made a detour before he could finish the thought.

Rachel took his hand in hers and pulled him to the floor. They knelt facing one another and Carlos watched his apartment vanish. Trees rose behind Rachel. Grass carpeted the floor. A new moon slashed a narrow thread of light in the darkness overhead. A soft, cool breeze wafted over his body. Wraith-like shapes hovered just within sight, circling around them.

Carlos knelt motionless as Rachel unbuttoned her blouse and removed her bra, releasing her breasts from confinement. The night wind played with her nipples, peaking them to attention, hard dark pebbles centered in luscious, glowing aureoles. A low chanting rose around him, a pulsing rhythm of urgency that paced his increasing heartbeat.

Carlos raised his hand, wanting to touch, to caress, that lovely body so close to him. An ominous glint flashed from the blade he somehow held. He shook his head, rejecting the reality even as it closed down over him, entered him and made him its slave. And before him, stretched on the cool lush grass, lay not Rachel but Shelby. Beautiful, sweet, innocent Shelby. Drugged, naked, open and waiting. As all of them were. For Carlos to accept his own truth. Even as he shook his head in denial, he raised his hand and plunged the knife down. **(end of Past part)**

Now, years later, **(return to Present part)** Carlos stood on the ledge and remembered the ritual on the lawn under the moon, the blood that flowed thick and black, and shuddered. His strength, the very essence of who he was, had bled out that night, run down the hot blade of his knife and the cool blades of grass to contaminate the earth on which they stood. Along with Shelby's blood. Shelby's life.

Carlos stood on the ledge and faced the doorway, a dark silhouette against the harvest moon. Dianna and Frank surged onto the roof, stopped when they saw him teetering on the parapet. Melissa smacked into them when she raced out of the stairwell.

Carlos smiled at them and held his arms out to his sides.

"Please, Carlos, don't do this," Dianna pleaded. "It's stupid. And unnecessary."

"All life is stupid," Carlos said. "And unnecessary."

"Come on, bro." Frank took a step toward the parapet. Behind Carlos, trees rustled in the freshening breeze. "Let's talk about this."

"Nothing to talk about. Sayonara."

Carlos lifted his face to the moon and shut his eyes. The movement played with his equilibrium. He swayed forward and back. Then he stepped off the ledge and flew into oblivion, with Shelby's scream echoing in his ears. **(end of scene)**

That's how it's done. You begin with a scene set in present time. Then you go back to the past, to the key scene that informs and motivates the present scene, then return to the present scene and finish it.

READ: *Write Away* (George, 2004), Page 145-149: Introduction, Exercise and Objective

Exercise #3: The Present-Past-Present Scene

(Purpose of Exercise: To explore the Present-Past-Present Technique)

WRITE A SCENE BETWEEN one of your main characters (this is the POV character) and at least one other person that begins in the present, goes into the past and returns to the present. The scene in the past can be with all the same characters who are in the present part of the scene, or have just the POV character interacting with different characters.

You can rewrite the scene you have been working with, use a scene (or proposed scene) from a story you are working on, or create an entirely new scene for this exercise.

Remember, though, that the action contained within the past part of the scene **must** be the action that moves the present action forward. It cannot be disconnected from the present action but must lead into it.

Set your timer for **20 MINUTES** and begin writing now.

Lesson #4: Introducing a New Character with the Lead-In Technique

USING THE LEAD-IN TECHNIQUE is a great way to introduce a new character into your narrative. The Lead-in Technique is almost identical to the Cliff-hanger ending. In a Cliff-hanger ending, a chapter ends at a moment of high suspense and the next chapter diverges from that plotline and leaves it hanging for a chapter or two. With the Lead-in, instead of moving away from the suspense of the chapter ending and concentrating on one or more of the subplots in the next chapter, the writer uses the suspenseful ending to bring a new character into the story.

Like the "Past" part of the previous scene technique, the narrative introduction of the new character needs to be personal in nature and must connect in some way to the ongoing action of the story. It can't simply be the stuff you think is really fun about the character but that doesn't have any real place in the story. The revelations can take the form of a conversation, interior thoughts or a memory/flash back.

This technique of introducing a new character into the story has two aims:

1. **To interest the reader** in the new character by revealing something interesting about him/her on a personal or career level, and

2. **To connect the introduction** to the present action of the scene.

This second piece is especially critical. The revelations about the new character **must tie into the present action**, even if only peripherally. If they don't tie in, then the information is merely reader-feeder and you run the risk of boring the reader, or losing their attention.

We've all read books that cross this line, by writers who couldn't resist the urge to include tidbits from their characters' biographies that they feel are immensely interesting even though they have no connection to the story itself. We scratch our heads and wonder why we need to know that Danny always wore a red undershirt in grade school, or Marie stores her canned goods upside down. We spend time wondering what that has to do with why Danny stole Herman's car, or Marie wants to adopt a Chinese baby, instead of paying attention to what is really happening in the story. And because the human mind cannot abide a mystery, our efforts will go into discovering the reason why these esoteric details are included, instead of enjoying the real story.

If you choose all your details with caution and care you will make sure your readers don't get sidetracked when reading your stories. And being detail-conscious will serve you especially well when using the Lead-in Technique to introduce a new character.

Here's what the Introducing a New Character with the Lead-in Technique looks like, from my paranormal suspense novel-in-progress with the working title *Tattooed In Death*.

(End of Previous chapter) Mackenzie took one look at the huge bear of a man strolling through the door and knew he was trouble. Major trouble.

(Beginning of next chapter, where the new character is introduced and his career and personality is revealed) Carrick Dunwitty walked into the pet shop with a chip on his shoulder. He'd wanted to haul the woman into the station and ream her a new one, but cooler—and, to him, more cowardly—heads had prevailed. He and Ackey were to observe only, and report back to the Lieutenant. Wheel spinning, that's what he was doing, since the bitch wasn't about to torture and kill her next victim on the front countertop. She'd need privacy for that—and soundproofing. Dunwitty felt like chewing someone up. Too bad it wouldn't be her—yet.

Rookie detective Carlos Soto had brought in the evidence two days ago, obtained, incredibly, from his firefighter brother-in-law, Norman Dunlap. Dunlap's wife, it seemed, styled herself a writer, and the story was one handed out at her bi-weekly critique meeting. Dunlap told Soto, red-faced and looking like he wanted to sink through the floor, that he often read the pieces his wife brought home to critique. His way of unwinding after a long shift.

"It was only because we'd talked about the case that he recognized what the story meant," Soto said.

The Lieutenant turned his penetrating stare on Soto. Dunwitty braced himself for an explosion.

"Not the details, Loo," Soto said, withering a bit beneath the weight of Lt. Gorman's gaze. "I mean, not anything we haven't given the press. I'd never leak information, not even to my wife."

Jonas Ackey elbowed Dunwitty in the side and shot him an amused grin. It was so much fun watching someone else roast on Gorman's spit.

"Get on with it," the Lieutenant growled.

"Si. I mean, yes. Uh, Sir." Soto swallowed and took a deep breath. "We'd hashed over theories on the perp at dinner the night before, so it was fresh in Norm's mind. It just seemed too much of a coincidence that someone would write a story about a murder that happened almost exactly the same way as a real one." He looked up and gave the senior detectives an owlish blink from behind his thick lenses. "I agreed, so Norm gave it to me. When I read about the stuff we kept back, the red scarf and the tattoo… Well…" He'd shrugged with both hands and shoulders. "I thought you needed to see it."

"Good thinking," Gorman said, and dismissed the junior detective back to his regular duties: investigating robberies. Then he looked at his homicide men. "You agree with the kid?"

Dunwitty looked down at his copy of the story.

"She did it," he said. "Or she's an accomplice."

"A damned stupid one," Jonas Ackey added, "to write something like this and think no one would recognize it for what it is. A confession."

"Mackenzie Straite," Dunwitty read from the top of the sheet —what Soto had explained was called a 'header,' whatever that meant. "Let's go get the bitch."

"Now hold on, here," Lt. Gorman had said. "We need her background first. And we need more than a simple fiction story to haul someone's ass in here for questioning. I'm not," he held up a hand to stop Dunwitty's red-hot protest, "saying we ignore this. But it doesn't seem like a woman's kind of crime, considering the amount of semen we found. And if she's an accomplice, which is what appears to be the case, then let's not spook the guy by grabbing her too fast."

"So what, then?" Dunwitty asked. By this time the entire office looked bathed in red to him. Ackey placed a hand on his arm, an action that moderated Dunwitty's temper just enough so that he only thought but didn't say aloud, *We wait until another girl dies before we get off our asses and do something?*

"I want you two to observe her. Don't interact, just observe. Watch her body language, see who she meets, who she talks with, where she goes. I'll get Bennett to do a thorough background and then we'll pull her in." Gorman pierced Dunwitty with his iron glare. "Capice?"

Dunwitty had nodded, thoroughly unhappy with sitting on the sidelines for even a couple of days. It was just not his nature to panty-waist around and 'observe.' But orders were orders, even stupid ones. And so he found himself with his partner at Los Osos Pets & Such, where the bitch worked part time. Dunwitty hated pets, annoying filthy critters that ran underfoot and ruined your possessions. And pet shops were full of the furry, feathery and scaley beasts, along with the rancid smells of suspicious foodstuffs, urine and feces. **(End of introduction; scene continues from here with Dunwitty as main character)**

So that's it. You end one chapter on a suspenseful note, then introduce a new character at the beginning of the very next chapter, right where the action ended, and go on from there. Of course, not all characters will be introduced this way; only those who will play a major role in the story would be eligible for this treatment, and probably only one or maybe two will actually merit a place in this particular scene structure. But it will definitely make your reader sit up and take notice of the new character and the information revealed about him/her when you use the Lead-in Scene.

READ: Write Away (George, 2004) page 149-150

Exercise #4: Introducing a New Character Via the Lead-In Technique

(Purpose of Exercise: To explore introducing a new character with the Lead-in technique)

WRITE THE ENDING LINE of a scene, or take the ending of one you have already written and work with that. Either jump forward in time no more than a few hours, or switch locations, and base the new scene on the action of the scene that has just ended.

In this new scene, you will be introducing a new character into the ongoing action. Take the time to let the reader know a bit about this new person, perhaps something about his or her personal life (spouse, children), background (how he/she grew up), or career (how he/she became who they are).

Remember your two aims in this kind of introduction: 1) to interest the reader in the new character by revealing something interesting about him/her, and 2) connecting the introduction to the present action of the scene, even if only peripherally.

When you have finished the introduction of the character, begin writing the action of the scene. Set your timer for **20 MINUTES** and start writing.

Lesson #5: The In Media Res Scene

IN MEDIA RES MEANS in "the middle of the action." This is the type of scene that can start a story or book with a real bang. It pulls the reader along because of the inherent excitement and suspense packed into the scene, and doesn't let go until the end. That is a real advantage when trying to interest a reader in your story.

One of the drawbacks to using an In Media Res scene to open a story is that the reader hasn't yet had time to get to know and bond with the main characters. The writer runs the real risk of the reader saying, "So what? Who cares?" and putting the book down unfinished.

In an In Media Res scene, when the character is introduced the action begins. There's no "getting to know you" period, no narrative, no advance scene setting, only action that drives the story forward. We stay with the character in the action, and where setting is introduced—as it must be in order to ground and orient the reader—it is done so as part of the action and not separate from it.

When using an In Media Res scene anywhere in your narrative, and **especially** when using it to open a story or book, you can't just write action alone. Not even if the In Media Res scene is somewhere other than the opening.

You still need to work carefully to include all those things that make characters and settings real to readers, and that help readers bond to the characters.

Judicious use of internal thoughts is a great way to do this, because readers get a look inside the POV character's head and heart and can understand the impact the action has on his/her life. The way the character interacts with other characters and the setting, and reacts to the action happening all around, can also reveal a lot about the character and create that all-important reader/character bond.

Here's a scene from my in-progress paranormal detective novel, with the current title *Tattooed in Death*.

> "I am not doing this!" Mackenzie glared at Ehler. "You can't make me." **(Scene opens in the middle of the action; we do not know what it is she doesn't want to do until the scene unfolds)**
>
> "Of course not. That's not my intention."
>
> Ehler's calm, rational voice infuriated her and she wanted to hit him. But how did one whack a blob of ectoplasm? And who would want that slime coating their fingers?
>
> "If you want to continue suffering, go ahead," he added. "You have my permission."
>
> "And you have my permission to go jump in a lake. A deep one."
>
> "Mackenzie," Amanda murmured. "Why not try it? It might work. Don't you want this to end?"
>
> Mackenzie stared at her best friend seated on the couch beside her, who seemed to have gone over to the dark side. But damn, she made sense. Mackenzie took a deep breath, squelched

her impulse toward phantomicide—was that even illegal?—and looked at Ehler.

"Okay, Fishman. Have it your way."

"Good." Ehler smiled, a tight, smug moue of his lips that narrowed Mckenzie's eyes. Before she could react he spoke again. "Close your eyes. Relax."

Mackenzie snapped her lids into a scrunch and tried to unball her fists. Ehler sighed.

"Mackenzie, please. At least try. Lean back and relax, just close your eyes, don't screw them shut. Give it a chance."

Mackenzie unclenched her jaw long enough to sigh. She leaned back against the couch cushions. That it was her living room, her possessions, that surrounded her helped only a little. Amanda took her hands and stroked them. Mackenzie felt her fingers uncurl and finally her shoulders dropped and the hard ball in the pit of her stomach loosened. Amanda held her hands in a gentle grip, and the warmth radiating from her flesh relaxed Mackenzie even further.

"That's good," Ehler murmured. "Now, send your mind out. Look for the Tattooer. Fix your attention on him, keep looking…"

Fishman's voice faded from her consciousness. Colors swirled behind her lids; a fist of pain jabbed at her left temple. Mackenzie held her breath and turned her head away, seeking escape, but Ehler's voice soothed her, talked her away from the beating tempo until it faded. A room emerged from the rushing eddy of color, dark and ominous. She could see wood walls stained with mildew and splotched with, oh, God, was that blood? She caught her breath.

"Find him, Mackenzie," Ehler urged in a soft whisper. "Find him and discover who he is."

She felt herself move, felt a warm darkness surround her, devour her. A shudder shook her body and suddenly she felt detached from herself. She rode uneasily inside another body, hard and foreign. A mind flew at her, battering at her like broken glass.

"It hurts," she whimpered, twisting in Amanda's hands.

"Control it," Fishman ordered. "Step away from the pain. It isn't yours, Mackenzie, it's his. Step away from the pain, but stay with him."

Mackenzie took a deep breath and lowered the shield she'd fashioned to isolate her from the killer's madness. Then she stepped fully inside him.

She looked down. Hands, strong, square, winding a rope into a noose. Dark hair on the knuckles, wide nails on spatulate fingers. They slowed, stopped. His/her head lifted, looked around the room. She saw the hook depended from the main ceiling beam, the handcuffs dangling from it. A wood floor splintered and stained, strewn with rubbish and torn clothing. An old iron bed squatted in one corner, an indistinct figure impaled on the mattress.

The body she rode in moved. She felt the legs stride to a sink in the corner. The hands turned on the water. The body bent and water cascaded over skin that felt thick with stubble. Once, twice.

He/she stood bent over the basin, water dripping from his face. Then he straightened up, raised his eyes to the mirror.

"Come on," Mackenzie whispered. "Let me see your face."

His eyes met hers in the mirror. She caught a glimpse of dark hair, a square face, a scar—where, on the jaw?—then evil flooded over her. He smiled.

"Gotcha!" he muttered.

Mackenzie yanked her hands from Amanda's and sat up with a scream. The vision shattered and she was once again in her own living room. Her heart thudded so hard she feared it would burst into tiny pieces. She looked at Bass Ehler.

"Oh, my God!" she said. "He saw me. He knows who I am!"

You can see from this example that there's no stopping to describe the setting, or the background of the character. We learn about Mackenzie's feelings from her internal thoughts, thoughts that are triggered by the action. The little we learn about the setting from the action allows us to understand we are in Mackenzie's house, in her living room. She's sitting with a friend on her own couch. That's all we need to know for this scene. Any further description of the room or of Mackenzie or her friend Manda, or even the ectoplasmic Ehrler, would only slow down the action. And yet it is just enough for readers to see the setting and to bond with Mackenzie because they understand her feelings.

READ: Write Away (George, 2004) page 150-152

Exercise #5: The In Media Res Scene

(Purpose of Exercise: To explore the In Media Res technique)

WRITE A SCENE THAT starts in the middle of the action. You can rewrite a scene you have used for a previous exercise, write a scene for a story you are currently working on, or create an entirely new scene for this exercise. You can have one, two or more characters in this scene, as you need.

Concentrate on the **action** in this scene. Keep the action going. Don't stop to describe either the character or characters, or the setting. Use internal thoughts to help the reader bond with the point of view character, and make sure the thoughts are connected to the action. When you need to reference the setting, be sure to make it a part of the action. Don't over-describe; give only as much as the reader needs to be able to visualize where the action is taking place.

Stay with the main character and the action throughout the entire scene. Don't slip into any of the other scene constructions.

Give yourself **20 MINUTES** to write this scene, starting now.

Lesson #6: The From Mind to Action Scene

SOMETIMES WE NEED A scene that gives the reader a break of sorts, a place to breathe a bit after a lot of action and/or tension. Or we need to deepen the connection between readers and the point of view character. We can't simply insert a cute little scene of a picnic in the park with the character's niece and nephew, who play no role in the story, just because we need to slow things down, or we'll lose our readers. And we can't impart fun little facts about our character's past that don't connect to the main plot. So what can we do to provide breathing room while maintaining forward motion and increasing the reader/character bond?

The From Mind to Action Scene serves this purpose perfectly. It eases the reader into the action of the next scene instead of jumping directly into it. It offers a quieter way to begin the scene that will afford the break, or breathing room, readers need periodically, while maintaining the tension and forward movement of the story. At the same time, it will help to deepen the connection between readers and character, because they will spend a longer period of time inside the character's head and heart.

The key is making sure that **everything is connected to the action** that has already happened before the scene starts and/or is about to happen as the scene unfolds. In the From Mind to Action Scene we start with the scene's point of view character and stay with that character all the way through. We get inside the character's head and heart, so that we know not just what the character does and says, but also what the character thinks and believes. Any setting description is given through the point of view character and is connected to that character in some way. Each detail is something that character would recognize and notice. Everything else doesn't exist.

We stay with and inside this character through this quiet period and on into the action as the scene continues to unfold. Done properly, a From Mind to Action Scene can make readers feel they truly know the character, his/her thoughts, hopes, dreams, aspirations and flaws. Empathy rises and readers have to continue reading to discover what will happen to this "new friend" they've met.

Here's what this scene looks like as it begins, from writing that I did with my class when we explored this lesson. It uses a character from my YA Unification series, which is still in progress. Emril is the male protagonist of the series. This won't be used in the book because his character has grown in a different direction by this point in the story and he's no longer as timid and fearful, but it is a good example of how a From Mind to Action Scene begins.

> Emril didn't want to be here, but somehow he couldn't stop his feet once they started to move. **(Start in the character's mind)** The dark stone closed tight around him, the unlit corridor barely wider than his shoulders. Shadows flittered from his small torch,

sending his gaze skittering over the dark rock, chasing phantom movement. His head brushed the ceiling in places, the ponderous weight of the earthen depths above like hands pressing on his shoulders. He wanted to turn, to flee back to his small cottage, to remain invisible and anonymous. He kept going.

He wasn't particularly brave. To be honest, he had no courage at all. It had been beaten out of him when his mother had been taken, banished by hard fists that had left him broken and bloodied on the floor. So what was he doing here now, inching his way toward certain destruction? If only he hadn't seen the girl in the mirror. If only he hadn't seen the words on her lips—help me—the same words he'd seen on his mother's lips before the Regent had smashed their mirror lifeline into lethal shards. But he had seen her, and now he felt trapped.

His heart thudded at the thought of calling attention to himself, but Hag Nacka had told him his destiny would be found in a mirror. And the girl was in the mirror. Emril had wanted more than anything to break the damned thing, but it was all he'd had left of his mother. So he'd covered it, thinking if he couldn't see in it, couldn't see what it contained, his future was safe. He growled now at the thought of how stupid he'd been.

A noise, small and high-pitched, stopped his feet. His heart ratcheted up into his throat and thundered so loudly it sounded to him like it echoed from the rock around him. He pressed against the stone and held his breath. Shadows flickered, insubstantial, then a dark, very substantial form hurtled out of the darkness, screeching in fear, hugging the floor. Emril kicked out at it as it passed; his boot connected with the form and sent it sailing in the air. It whacked into the wall opposite him and lay still. Emril shone the torch on it. A rat. He shuddered and again wished he could turn back.

But this girl needed him. She had to be important if she could use the mirror. His mother had told him only feys and witches and the E'olun knew the secret magic. He'd denied and dithered for days before his feet took the decision out of his hands. Now, here he was. He'd do his duty and get her out of the aerie, deliver her to the Forest and let her go her own way. And he'd go his. He wasn't brave, he had no courage and he wasn't about to find any now, at this late date. He hadn't saved his mother and he wasn't interested in saving anyone else. But he knew one cannot fight destiny. So he'd go only as far as he had to, and no further.

The tunnel branched. The left side ended twenty yards away. The right side rose in a series of steps. Emril again cursed his life; if only he'd died with his mother, he'd not be facing this now. Oh, well, he thought as he turned left and edged up the steps. *Maybe I won't survive this, anyway.* The thought gave him little comfort. Especially when he reached the top of the steps and the air exploded around him. **(full action of the scene begins here)**

As you can see, we stay in Emril's head all the way through the opening of this scene, as he inches his dangerous way to where the girl is being held prisoner. We learn a lot about shy, timid Emril in this From Mind to Action scene, who he is, what kind of person he is, and the lies and half-truths he tells himself. Readers want to know what will happen to him, if he will be successful in rescuing the girl, and if he will find his courage at last or simply leave her on her own in the forest.

READ: Write Away (George, 2004) page 152-154

Exercise #6: The From Mind to Action Scene

(Purpose of Exercise: To explore the From Mind to Action Scene)

CRAFT A SCENE THAT starts in the point of view character's head, goes into a short description of setting, and then moves into action as filtered through the POV character's mind.

Remember that since this scene starts in your character's mind, it will lean heavily on what the POV character thinks and feels about the setting, action and other characters all throughout the scene, especially in the beginning, rather than concentrating on either the setting or action.

Rewrite one of the scenes you've already created, or make up an entirely new scene for this exercise. Or create a scene in the From Mind to Action technique for a story you're presently working on.

Set your timer for **15 MINUTES** and begin writing.

Lesson #7: Dramatic Narration

SCENES DO NOT ALL have to be action. Sometimes you will find a specific place where you want to let the reader know what happens, but you don't need a full scene. Perhaps it's the dialogue that won't work for any number of reasons, the most common being that the dialogue doesn't add anything to the forward movement of the story. Perhaps what is said would be trite and boring in a full scene. Perhaps it is what happens that is important, not what is said. Or perhaps only a portion of what happens in the scene is truly important, and the rest is merely fluff that adds volume without substance.

Whatever the reason, a full scene with setting, dialogue and character interactions won't work. But you still have important information that the reader must have at this point, information that moves the story forward and without which the story stands still. What do you do?

Insert a Dramatic Narration Scene. Technically speaking, this is not an actual scene showing what happens as it unfolds. It is the narrator **telling** the reader what happens. This allows the narrator to "truncate," if you will, the action and dialogue through the POV character into only those elements that are necessary for the movement of the story.

Yes, in general the rule of thumb is to show, not tell. But there are times when it is more dramatic, and has more impact, when you tell and don't show. Times when showing becomes tedious and/or superfluous.

In a Dramatic Narration Scene there is **no dialogue**. The narrating character tells what happens from his/her own point of view. Still, the characters in a Dramatic Narration Scene grow and learn, inner and outer conflicts develop, and other tools such as figurative language are used.

Here is what a Dramatic Narration Scene looks like. I wrote this in one of my classes in which we explored writing a Dramatic Narration Scene. The first line of the scene was the given opening line of the exercise.

> He always read the paper a day late. It gave his wife and daughter time to riffle through it, express their horror at man's inhumanity to man, drool over juicy bits of gossip gleaned from between the lines, exclaim in delight at proffered sales around the county. And the wait sharpened his own expectation. He could feel his pulse begin its gradual rise, his heartbeat slow to a ponderous thud that hailed what he had long called 'A Possible.' Everything awaited him while he awaited his turn at the paper. There wasn't always A Possible in each paper, but the anticipation was delicious in itself.
>
> Selma and India had no idea why he held himself aloof from the paper the day it arrived. They laughed at him, at his insistence that the pages needed to breathe, to lose the cloying scent of dank

ink, before he could lose himself in the daily travails of the town. He told them that fresh ink gave him a headache. He wasn't sure they believed him, but the fact that they had the upper hand in this one little aspect of their lives kept them from asking any intrusive questions. They simply obliged by taking the paper onto the sun porch while they perused it, so the ink wouldn't set off one of his 'spells,' as Selma called them.

He'd instituted the spells within a few weeks of their marriage, to guarantee himself privacy and isolation from Selma's omnipresence. Shifting them to include the paper proved a serendipitous bonus. All he asked was that they leave the paper as they'd found it: each page in pristine order, each section tucked into the others, the folded issue returned to its plastic sheath. At first, he'd allowed Selma to cut out the coupons and sale ads that caught her eye, but when he'd lost out on A Possible that had been printed on the back of a Macy's ad, he'd almost lost control. He'd regained his senses just in time. Selma had spent two days in the hospital instead of eternity in a coffin, and she'd never mutilated the paper again.

He picked up yesterday's edition, let his fingers caress the smooth clear plastic while a shiver traversed his spine. Then he slid the folded pages from the narrow bag and spread them out on his desktop. He knew neither wife nor daughter would interrupt him, not during his paper reading time. They had learned better, both of them.

He ran his hands over the slick surface as he read, the pages a soft body beneath his questing fingers, his brain chanting, let it be, let it be, as his eyes devoured the print. Then his heart stopped. There it was, on page 24, section B: A Possible. A life he could truly devour, a body he could truly own. An innocent who would soon learn the ways of his dark and tangled world.

Smiling, he refolded the paper, rose and left the house, the address reverberating in his head.

Dramatic Narration allows writers to cut out any extraneous parts of the story and hone in on the truly important. What was said by this man, his wife and his daughter concerning the paper and its state when he read it, is not important. Nor is the actual abuse he dealt out to his wife, only the fact that he did abuse her. It is the man's view of his life and the role the paper plays in it that is important to the story. To include all the minutiae of his daily interaction with wife and daughter would take the spotlight off his aberration and the menace embedded in his leaving the house. It would be a different story altogether if Dramatic Narration were not used here.

Exercise #7 that follows will allow you to experience this type of scene. And in the next two exercises, we will explore two variations on the Dramatic Narration Scene—Narrative Summary and Interrupted Dramatic Narration.

READ: Write Away (George, 2004) page 129-133

Exercise #7: Dramatic Narration

(Purpose of Exercise: To explore dramatic narration)

WRITE A SCENE USING Dramatic Narration only, where the narrator tells what happens instead of the characters acting it out.

This is a full scene, just like any other, only done in narration style. The characters will grow and develop. Inner and outer conflicts will arise. But there will be **no dialogue**. For this exercise, keep to one point of view (POV) throughout. Let the narrator, through this point of view character, tell what happens instead of letting all the characters act it out.

Set your timer for **20 MINUTES** and begin writing.

Begin your scene with: She (he) never wore red in the evening.

Lesson #8: Narrative Summary

NARRATIVE SUMMARY IS A short form of Dramatic Narration. Characters do **not** grow and develop in Narrative Summary. Action is kept to a minimum. The events are narrated as quickly and economically as possible. While technically not a true scene, when well done it often feels like a little mini-scene that bridges two full scenes.

Narrative summary is a great device to use when you need to move your character or characters from one place to another, or from one time period to another, but nothing of great import happens on the journey through space or time. Narrative summary can create a specific atmosphere, be used to develop symbols and symbolic threads, and introduce a major change less abruptly than a simple line break (which is often used to show the passage of time, a change in setting, or a change in point of view character) without alluding to the change. Narrative summary allows the writer to employ **a paragraph or two** to drop clues, create atmosphere or deepen interest without boring or confusing readers.

In this example from work I did in one of my classes, Julia, who lives in the city, goes out into the country to find the isolated cabin in the woods owned by the man who has been threatening her. I used three short paragraphs of narrative summary to show Julia's journey through the woods to the cabin, a journey that, had it taken any longer, would have probably bored readers to death. The fourth paragraph begins the action of the coming full scene.

Dark clouds hid the moon, which would have given her enough light to see the path. **(Summary used to move Julia to the setting)** Julia did have a flashlight with her, but turning it on would advertise her presence, and she wasn't sure who else was out in the woods with her—except for deer and possums or other nocturnal animals. But she wasn't afraid of them. It was the two-legged variety that frightened her these days.

The old cabin had to be nearby, she'd been stumbling in the dark for almost fifteen minutes. Generally in an easterly direction, because she hadn't strayed from the path too often. Soft noises erupted in front of her and she froze, listening, eyes closed to make the sounds clearer. After a moment, she realized it was a deer pulling leaves from a bush, and she relaxed enough to flick on the light, filtering it through her fingers. Yes, she was near the cabin, maybe 500 feet away now.

She lowered the light and it glinted on an object half-hidden beneath a lush fern. She stooped and picked it up, turned it over beneath the light. A shoe. Red and silver, ankle straps and a high platform sole. Almost pristine condition, certainly not here from before the last rainstorm. A week at most. Angelica's shoe.

(**Action begins**) Angelica—she had been out here, on the path? At the cabin? Julia's heart stood still. This changed everything. Heedless now of the light, she strode on toward the cabin.

That is how Narrative Summary works. One to three or four short paragraphs of "from here to there," or "from then to now" or "from Character A to Character B" that move the story from where the last scene ended to where it needs to be to continue. In it we learn more about Julia, discover an important clue (Angelica's shoe), and are steeped in an eerie, threatening atmosphere. All this draws the reader on into the full scene that follows.

Exercise #8: Narrative Summary

(Purpose of Exercise: To explore the use of narrative summary)

USING NARRATIVE SUMMARY, WRITE a short mini-scene that summarizes the action instead of drawing it out into a full scene. The purpose of this mini-scene is to either move the character(s) from one place to another, move the story from one time frame to another, or to impart important information that moves the story along, perhaps even pushing it in a different direction. It can also be used to create a specific atmosphere of menace, fear, despair, hopelessness, etc.

Keep this narrative Summary to from one to four **short** paragraphs only. Try to inject a sense of rising tension into the narration, and a twist or lead-in to the full scene that will follow.

Give yourself **10 MINUTES** to create this short Narrative Summary passage.

Lesson #9: Interrupted Dramatic Narration

THERE MAY BE TIMES when you don't need a full scene to convey information, but you need more than dramatic narration. These are cases where one nugget of information and the characters who deliver it—or how they deliver it—are critical to the story movement, but the larger scene in which it is contained is of no real consequence and would merely slow down the story and bore or confuse readers.

So, how do you handle this kind of situation? How do you render a scene with setting and dialogue when you are in the midst of dramatic narration? By inserting a partial scene **within** the dramatic narration: Interrupted Dramatic Narration.

The partial scene is a short form of a full scene, but only addresses the one main point that needs to be imparted to the reader. You start with dramatic narration, telling the reader what is happening, then segue into the partial scene that shows the reader the action and dialogue, then dive back into dramatic narration to finish the scene.

Here's what it looks like, from a piece I wrote during one of my classes. We're again with Julia from the last exercise, only earlier in the story.

Julia stood at the window, watching the moon slide in and out of rents in the clouds. **(narrative—telling what is happening—opens the scene)** The garden appeared limned in skeletal light, then vanished into an inky cauldron. Nothing moved out there that she could see. Nothing beckoned to her to come out, to meet a fate known only to the ghostly presence that awaited her. Tonight, the garden appeared safe.

Perhaps she should go out there where it was safe. If anywhere was safe for her these days. She could hear the faint stirrings in the house: boards creaking, walls shifting, air currents sighing, and she wondered who was abroad this time. Who had come to disturb the peace the ignorant masses in the city believed she reveled in.

She turned from the window and closed the curtain, then snapped on the bedside lamp. She didn't know why she stood in the dark, longer each night than the night before. Soon, she'd stand unlit all through the long, endless nighttime hours. She knew she was tempting fate, asking the ghosts to return. As if they ever roamed when she was expecting them. That, she knew, was the point. To come when she least expected it, to catch her unawares, to slowly drain the sanity from her mind, the energy from her body, until she became one of them. An evil wraith, haunting the scene of the crime.

But not her crime. Julia clung to that slippery conviction, arms aching from the strain of holding to the facts as she remembered them. Except now she wasn't sure she could trust her memories. She'd had physical proof, a printed report of the jury verdict, but it had vanished a month ago—at least she thought it was a month, but time, too, was slipping away from her —and now all she had left was the remembered sound of the courtroom that last, fateful day. **(beginning of partial scene)**

"Hold on, Jules, this is it," her lawyer whispered as they stood and faced the jury box. None of the jurors would look at her and a strange, dead numbness spread out from her heart. "Keep your head high and let them see you, see what this means to you."

"What does it mean?" she asked, but her voice was too low for him to hear and so he didn't answer. Or he ignored her, which he had gotten good at doing over those few months.

"We the jury," the foreperson read in a nasal tone, a man in his mid-fifties who obviously over-loved Italian food, "in the above titled action, murder in the first degree, do find Julia Marie Langston not guilty." He looked up, straight into Julia's eyes and announced his disgust to the reporters and spectators who filled the courtroom. "Unfortunately." **(end of partial scene; narration resumes)**

And so Julia had been released to return to where her parents had been slaughtered, to live in shadow-haunted rooms through guilt-laden nights. Now, she drifted out into the upper hall toward the curving maple staircase, drawn by the sound of footsteps echoing in the lower hall. She didn't call out. She knew from experience that no one would answer. Because no one was there. Not anyone alive.

Moonlight glimmered on the satiny steps as she descended, her shadow a living presence wafting before her, blocking light to the archway into the parlor. She paused at the bottom of the steps, her hand clutching the banister. The sounds had moved, seemed to be coming from behind her. She forced herself not to look, terrified of what—who—she would see. Or see through, as the case might be.

A board creaked in the hallway, and Julia spun. Another creaked in the parlor and she lurched through the archway, her heart hammering in her chest. She wanted to call out, to ask who was there, but she was afraid of the answer. She wanted to turn on a light, but was afraid to move from the center of the room. Faint moans rode the air and she kept turning, seeking the room's corners, wanting answers, fearing what she was becoming, finding nothing but fear. Then a shape materialized out of the gloom beside the fireplace. It stalked closer and closer, hand outstretched to capture and consume her.

"Daddy?" Julia whispered. Icy fingers stroked her cheek. Her mind rebelled and she fell into a deep dark abyss. **(end of scene)**

The partial scene can be short, as this one is, or longer, with more characters and dialogue involved. The important thing to remember is that it must contain only that one nugget of important action or dialogue that needs to be fully rendered, and must be sandwiched, "bookended" as it were, in between two portions of a dramatic narration scene.

READ: *Write Away* (George, 2004) Page 135 (bottom) – 139 (top)

Exercise 9: Interrupted Dramatic Narration

(Purpose of Exercise: To learn to insert a partial scene
into dramatic narration)

USING THE SCENE YOU just wrote, or starting with a fresh scene, write
an Interrupted Dramatic Narration Scene: that is, a scene that starts out as
Dramatic Narration, goes into a Partial Scene and ends with Dramatic
Narration. The Dramatic Narration portions will not contain any dialogue.
The Partial Scene will contain dialogue, but once the salient points have
been rendered, the Dramatic Narration will take over again. What you will
have, in essence, is dramatic narration, a pause for dialogue within an
unspecified scene, and then a return to narration.

Set your timer for **20 MINUTES** and start writing your interrupted
dramatic narration scene.

Lesson #10: The Scene Question

JUST AS EVERY STORY has a story question, so every scene in the story has its own scene question. When the scene question is made clear at the beginning of the scene, readers will continue to read to discover the answer to the question. It is the need to know that pulls readers on from one scene to the next.

The scene question is tied to the structure of the scene. To be effective, scenes need to be structured in a specific way. This structure is based on **conflict**. You have **two characters with opposing goals**. This sets them into conflict. The first character states his/her goal at the beginning of the scene: "This is what I will achieve." The second character, whose goal opposes that of the first character's, says in effect, "Oh, no you won't because I want something else." And the fight ensues, either physically in an action scene, or verbally in a dialogue scene. And the reader turns pages, worrying about whether the first character will win, or whether the second character will be successful in achieving his/her aims.

This worry on the part of the reader is the protagonist's goal expressed as a question. This is called the **Scene Question**. Just as every story has a Story Question (see *Workbook #1: Character, Setting, Story*) every scene has its own scene question, and it **must be answered** by the time the scene ends. The scene question is what the reader asks and worries about and is almost always a "yes" or "no" question: Will Mark pass the test? Will Amy forget the words to the song? Will Abner keep his class in order? Will the detective find the next clue to solve the murder?

However, the scene question for each scene—until the final one—must be answered **badly**, or you will lose tension, urgency and the reader. If each scene ends with everyone happy and all problems solved, there is no reason for readers to continue with the story because they have nothing to worry about. On the other hand, if the answer to the scene question makes things worse and leads to another scene question that also makes things worse, and so on through the story, readers **will have to read on to find out** if the heroes will prevail in the end.

Scene questions, until the final scene, cannot be answered with an unqualified "yes." The usual answer is "no." But they don't always have to be answered with an **"unqualified no."** They also can be answered with what I call a **"qualified yes."** That is, the "yes" answer to the question leads to a bigger problem than if the answer was a simple "no."

For instance, take the first scene question above: Will Mark pass the test? You could simply have him fail the test—an "unqualified no." Or he could pass the test, only to discover one of the students obtained a copy ahead of time and the teacher invalidated the test—a "qualified yes." Or: Will the detective find the next clue to solve the murder? The answer can be "no," and he continues his search with time running out for the next victim. Or it can be a "qualified yes," where he finds the clue but the murderer sees him find it and then goes after the detective's family.

However you answer the scene question, with an "unqualified no" or a "qualified yes," each succeeding scene must pose **a more serious question**, one that leads to greater tension and suspense (for more on creating tension and suspense, see *Workbook #5: Conflict/Tension; Style*). And each answer to the scene question must put the character in worse shape than before. Basically, you get your protagonist up in a tree (a dilemma), then start throwing rocks (problems) at him to get him down again. Each rock (problem) is bigger than the next until he gets knocked out of the tree and has to deal with and solve the problems.

Here, in a nutshell, is the Scene Question Structure:

1. Pose a scene question by stating Character A's goal clearly as a question (can be inferred by the reader).
2. Put Character B's goal in direct conflict with Character A's goal.
3. Let the characters "fight it out" either physically or verbally, starting small and getting bigger and more serious as the scene develops.
4. Craft a disastrous answer to the scene question to end the scene —either an "unqualified no" or a "qualified yes."

This example of how the scene question-and-answer works is from an exercise I did in one of my classes. I used characters from *Destany's Daughter*, the first in my YA Unification Quadrilogy, when I was just beginning to work on the book. This first draft was eventually expanded and split into two separate scenes: Meleia trying to escape what became her cell in the aerie dungeon, and meeting the brother she didn't know she had. In the final version, there is no door or lock to Meleia's cell, only a magical forcefield keeping prisoners caged.

Scene Question: Will Meleia escape from the room where she's being held captive?

There has to be a way out, Meleia thought as she scrutinized the room. (Meleia's scene goal)

Transparent walls showed nothing outside but darkness dotted with distant points of light. She wasn't sure if they were stars, or other rooms like hers. The smooth stone floor was bare of carpet. The only furnishing was the bed on which she sat. She'd already explored the bathroom, which held nothing that could help her: no towels, no razor, no cans of hairspray. All she had was a bar of soap, a tube of toothpaste, a toothbrush, a roll of toilet paper, the clothes on her back and the bed linens.

Maybe I could fashion a noose of sorts to strangle him with, she thought, fingering the thick top sheet, not sure she could even tear it into strips. A key scraped in the door lock and she looked up to find her captor staring at her. A malicious smile lit his face, as though he knew her thoughts and found them amusing.

"Are you enjoying your stay, my dear?" he asked, his voice a low purr.

Meleia stood and glared at him.

"You can't keep me here, Uncle."

"Really?" His smile widened. "You intend to stop me?" (Uncle's scene goal: to keep her imprisoned, inferred from his smile and his taunting words.)

He stepped into the room and Meleia sidled to her left. If she could get him far enough away from the door, maybe she could dart around him and be down the stairs before he realized what she was doing. She lowered her gaze, refusing to allow herself to so much as glance at the open door to freedom. She wanted to give him no inkling of her plan.

"If you want out, my dear, all you need do is cooperate."

"In your dreams, maybe."

Her uncle reached out as though to caress her cheek. Meleia jerked back and he laughed. He stalked toward her and again she backed away, pressing inch by tiny inch toward her goal.

"Your brother is anxious to see you, Meleia." A cruel smile curved his lips. "Don't you want to see him?"

Meleia stopped, shocked and confused. She searched his face, his eyes, hoping to find a glimmer of truth in them. But the hard obsidian-like orbs glittering in his face held only contempt.

"What brother?" She shook her head. "I don't have a brother."

"Of course you do. Didn't your mother tell you about him? How she left him behind with me when she ran off to the otherworld?"

He stepped closer, touched her cheek with gentle fingers. Meleia took two more steps toward the gaping portal.

"We're your family, Meleia," he crooned, his voice sugar warm. It stroked down her frazzled nerves, seeking to calm her. "We love you. We want you back with us. We've missed you so much. You belong here, with us. Don't you understand that?"

She wanted to believe him, wanted to believe he cared for her, wanted to believe her only uncle hadn't killed his own sister, her mother. Then she looked up into his eyes and saw the lie, saw her doom if she put herself into his hands.

"I hate you!" she screamed, and shoved him back with all her strength.

He stumbled toward the bed, arms flailing. She raced toward freedom, reached the portal and tried to slam the door shut behind her. But she couldn't catch the edge and couldn't slow down enough to try again. She grasped the railing and flung herself down, two, three, five steps. Then a hard hand dug into her hair and hauled her a stop, whirled her around and threw her up the steps. The stair edge caught her ribs and she lay gasping for breath. Her uncle picked her up and dragged her back into the room. He threw her up against the iron footboard and pinned her there, hands on her shoulders, his enraged face inches from hers. Pain tears blurred her vision as she struggled to break his hold. He bent and placed his lips on her ear.

"I will never let you go. Never!"

He hauled her upright and laid the back of his hand across her face. Then he dropped her on the hard uncompromising floor. The snap of the door lock echoed through the pain in Meleia's head. **(disastrous answer to scene question)**

As you can see, this scene question was answered with a resounding "unqualified no." Meleia did not escape from the room. In addition, she has learned the disturbing information that she has a brother, one her mother did not tell her about, a brother her mother supposedly abandoned as a baby. She knows now the lengths her uncle will go to force her to give him what he wants, even as far as beating her. The danger has increased, and her need to escape is now greater than before. Readers will continue worrying about her, and keep turning pages to discover if, or how, she will eventually escape.

READ: *The 38 Most Common Fiction Writing Mistakes* (Bickham, 1992) Page 61-63

Exercise #10: The Scene Question

(Purpose of exercise: to work with the Scene Question)

WRITE A SCENE BETWEEN two characters using the Scene Question Structure. (And remember, no matter which scene structure you use, all scenes will have a scene question.) Start by noting **at the top of the page** what the Scene Question is. State it as a yes-or-no question.

Then below that start the scene with the first character, stating the character's goal clearly. Now, bring in a second character whose goal conflicts with the first goal. State that opposing goal just as clearly.

Develop the scene moment-by-moment (with no summary, this is a full scene) until you reach the end. Make sure the end of the scene is **disastrous**; that is, it answers the Scene Question **badly,** with either an unqualified no or a qualified yes. This often means using a twist, surprise or unanticipated turning of the tables on the main character.

But remember, as in all truly satisfying stories, you need to plant clues (very subtle ones) that foreshadow the ending twist or surprise.

Now set your timer for **20 MINUTES**, note your scene question at the top of the page, and begin writing.

Lesson #11: The Transition

TRANSITIONS ARE SINGLE SENTENCES or whole paragraphs that link scenes together into a smooth narrative. Without a way to link scenes, the narrative will jump around and confuse readers. It will feel disjointed. Readers will wonder how the characters got to the setting in which the action takes place, or why they decided to take the train instead of a plane. They will wonder why they were with Mary in the last scene and now suddenly are with Bill. They will be confused that three years have passed in an instant without any reference to the passage of time. And they will spend time wondering and worrying about those inconsequential things instead of what is happening in the story itself.

Transitions come at both the beginning and the end of each scene, though the beginning transition is the most noticeable, for it orients readers to the change that has taken place between the previous scene and the present scene. Ending transitions conclude the scene by alerting readers that a change is coming, and are softer than opening transitions.

An ending transition (I call them "transition alerts" because they are not full transitions, but only let readers know one is coming up) that signals a coming change might look like this: "Christa thought about what the detective told her, then picked up her car keys and left the house." This signals that a change of setting will take place when the next scene begins. The opening transition that follows will find Christa either in her car, or at the place she has driven to, and will lead into the next scene.

Jordan Rosenfeld, in her wonderful book, *Make A Scene* (a Writer's Digest book), that details how to craft effective, unforgettable scenes, likens scenes to the different cells of the body. All are distinct and unique in themselves, but must work together to create a smooth, unified whole. It is transitions that allow the cells to unite seamlessly.

Opening transition paragraphs are similar to dramatic narrative, except that they don't contain any scenic elements. They simply connect scenes, so that the story takes on a cohesive shape. Transitions occur at the beginning and end of your scenes, places where you condense the narrative as you shift time, space, point of view, etc., as you bypass the boring and mundane events of your characters' lives.

This is an important point. As Jordan Rosenfeld writes in *Make A Scene*, "Fiction is a *simulation* of real life; your goal is to offer only the most meaningful, relevant and dramatic moments in your characters' lives..." You do this by bypassing anything that isn't meaningful, relevant and/or dramatic.

Transitions at the beginning of a scene will signal a change in **six** main ways. They alert readers that something has changed, and orient them in time, space, action, character, etc.

Use **beginning transitions** to signal:
1. A Change of Time
2. A Change of Location
3. A Change of Mood or Atmosphere

4. A Change of Point of View

5. A Plot Transition

6. A Character Transition

Here are how these types of transitions work in your story structure.

1. Change of Time: There are a number of devices you can use to alert readers to the passage of time. It can be as simple as a narrative sentence noting the time gap (Three years later, Amanda returned to the town where she grew up.), an opening line of dialogue ("I can't believe it's been a whole year since we met for coffee."), or a relation to time via setting (The open fields Neil remembered from his last visit were now covered with a network of suburban housing.). Or you can use a paragraph, or series of paragraphs, to condense the passage of time. This last is especially necessary when there has been a large gap in time. Readers will need to know relevant events that happened during that gap. Dramatic Narration used as a transition will let readers know what happened "off stage," as it were, and keep the plot continuous throughout the timeline of the story.

2. Change of Location: Again, the transition into a change of location can be a simple sentence (Bill's house was larger than Adelle's and she wondered how he could have filled up all that space.) or a paragraph or two that includes more detail of the new setting, and/or the journey from here to there.

This example is from my novella in-progress titled, "Dead Ringer," and shows the transition from the scene outside at the beach to the scene in the house.

> That's when I made my mistake. I shook my head and the universe tilted. My head exploded, my hands went numb and my legs buckled. I heard the gun hit the ground just about the time

Butter Voice's arms wrapped around my waist. I remember looking down and watching his feet recede into the distance before everything went dark again, and thinking, Spats? What the hell? **("Transition alert" at end of previous scene)**

I woke lying in a bed, but I knew it wasn't mine. **(beginning of transition into new scene)** The mattress was hard and lumpy, cracks crazed the ceiling and there was a dim light coming from my left. That herd of elephants still salsa danced in my head. I tried to convince myself it had all been just a dream, but there was too much evidence to the contrary, starting with the lingering smell of cigarette smoke. Definitely not my house.

I turned my head. Another mistake; my lunch almost landed on the bedspread. I pressed a hand to my temple, surprised that I wasn't tied to the bedposts; these guys obviously had no idea who they were dealing with. A man sprawled in a wicker chair to my left. Clues I didn't want to see leapt into view: the pleated, windowpane check suit pants with matching vest, the bow tie and spats, a fedora on the table beside him. Butter Voice. He was busy studying me as he ground out an unfiltered cigarette in the half-full ashtray that sat beneath a fringed lampshade. Shit, shit, shit. Not again, I thought as he sent a glare in my direction. **(end of transition into new scene)**

"Just who are you?" he asked. **(beginning of action)**

A transition like this is not license to describe everything in sight. Choose the details carefully, including only those that enhance the action and plot, reflect the character's personality or inner desires, impart necessary information, and/or serve as symbolic meaning. Allow the characters to interact with and/or react to the setting (as in the one-sentence example, Adelle's thoughts about Bill's house). You can also choose setting details that create a needed specific atmosphere or mood.

3. Change of Mood or Atmosphere: When the setting remains the same but you need to signal that there is a shift—a plot twist is coming or a character's attitude has changed—use a transition that shows a change in mood or atmosphere. Reflect the atmosphere of the setting or the inner world of the characters by using a change in the weather, sensory details like smell, touch, sound, etc., or jarring and/or juxtaposed elements that evoke an eerie or mystical feel, etc. Consider this transition paragraph from my short story, "The SomeWhen Murder":

> It was the same room I'd checked into a few hours earlier, and yet it wasn't. The old oak dresser no longer sat beside the door; clothing hung on pegs in its place. The lady's desk where I'd parked my laptop had vanished to make way for a dry sink complete with china ewer and basin. The wall sconces held candles, not bulbs, and the bedside reading lamp now sported a hurricane chimney, wick and clear liquid in a glass reservoir. The cabbage roses on the wall shimmered a brilliant maroon, and a braided rag rug replaced the worn Oriental knockoff on which I'd dropped my duffel. I realized that curtains did cover the window, but the filmy lace did little to cut the glare of sun on snow.

4. Change of Point of View: Moving from one character's point of view to another's is a great way to denote a change of scene. The key here it to make sure you identify the point of view character clearly **within the first sentence or two,** so that readers understand immediately that they have left one character for another. If the POV change is done within a chapter, a line break (blank space between the scenes) is usually used. Often, a point of view shift will occur at the start of a new chapter. But even if you use the new point of view character's name as part of the chapter heading—

Chapter One   Chapter Two

Gregory   Damien

—be aware that **most readers do not read chapter headings**. When they are immersed totally in a story (as you want them to be in yours), they turn pages and continue reading the text with little regard to chapter headings. So it is important to orient readers to the point of view character in the first sentence or two of each new scene and chapter, so they know whom they are reading about.

Here's an example of a change of point of view from within a chapter of my suspense novel, *Sins of the Past*. In the first part of the chapter we are with Mitch, the FBI agent. Then we have a line break and transition to Sabrina's point of view:

> Mitch stared at his unconscious assistant, pushing aside the knowledge that the young man had a wife and two small children back in Washington. He brooded on the puzzling actions of his cunning adversary and sipped the coffee without tasting it, eyes and ears alert, his weapon in hand, ready to fire. His ruminations brought him no closer to enlightenment. Far to the south a siren wailed, drew slowly closer. Another joined it. And not quite as far to the north, though Mitch did not know, a pair of high-intensity field glasses kept careful watch on the

increasing activity around Sabrina Steves Compton's summer cottage.

* * *

"Yes, Geoff, I have it on," Sabrina assured her worried friend. The muted voice from the radio on the desk warred with Geoff Simmonds' for her attention. Pressing the ancient receiver to her ear, she turned her back to the old, rounded oak box and gave her attention completely to Geoff.

5. Plot Transition: If an important event took place in the previous scene, or you are picking up the action after the cliff-hanger ending of the previous scene or chapter ending, or your character had an epiphany realization at the end of the last scene, you will want to open with a reference to that event or ending that shows where your character is at this point in relation to that ending. For example, if your character discovered a dead body, or the plane is spiraling out of control, or your character has just realized she loves her professor, you may need to let readers know how the character responds to that: calls the police; takes the pilot's place; decides to drop the class because he is married.

Here's an example from my in-progress sci-fi/fantasy novel, *Stealing Shyon*. There are 5 stories going at the same time, and each chapter ends on a cliff-hanger that puts one of 5 characters in danger. At the end of chapter fifteen, Queen Amalia was carried off by a gigantic bird. Chapter sixteen picks up a subplot concerning Amalia's sister, Karina. Chapter seventeen details the response of the outlaw Daigard to the Queen's capture. Then in chapter eighteen, we return to the Queen, orienting the reader immediately to the Queen's story by both naming her and mentioning the bird in the first sentence:

Amalia groaned and her eyes fluttered open when the bird laid her on the rough floor of its nest. It moved away and settled a few feet away from her, watching with bright beady eyes as she slowly sat up. She stared back, her heart stuttering with fear, until she finally realized that it was going to leave her alone. She turned her head and looked around.

6. Character Transition: When a character's inner response, his/her emotional response, to a previous scene is important, you may open the next scene with the character's thoughts or internal monologue on how his/her feelings are different than they were in the previous scenes.

Consider this example from my in-progress (untitled) sci-fi novel, which bridges the opening scene in a tavern with the scene that takes place in a deserted corner of Scumville:

> But perhaps the night needn't be a total loss. If he followed the girl and her companion, he just might uncover something useful: information such as how she had gotten to Scumville from Uf-fo's deus-city; why she was being helped by a government mole; how sympathetic she really was to the Faex's plight; where she had gotten her Faex clothing and identification papers; who the father was who would listen and do something. About what? Or was it who? Whatever the answers, Condor had a strong feeling they would prove important to the Movement.

In the first scene, all Condor wanted was to meet his contact and leave. He wasn't willing to take any further risks. But what he discovered in the tavern changed his view of what was happening and what it might mean to both him and the organization to which he belonged. He found himself experiencing an emotion he thought he had eradicated long ago, one he could not deny: curiosity. And that leads him into the second scene of the story.

<u>READ:</u> *Make A Scene* (Rosenfeld, 2008) Page 258-265

Exercise #11: The Transition

Combining Scenes Into A Smooth Narrative

USING THE SCENE YOU just finished in the last exercise, continue on in your story, choosing a different scene type (ex: if you used Motion Picture for the first scene, you might choose From Mind to Action or Present-Past-Present for the next scene.

Link the scenes with **no more than two or three paragraphs** of narrative transition. Keep the paragraphs fairly short. If there is a large break in time, try to incorporate some narrative summary into the transition paragraphs. Work to make the transition between scenes as smooth as possible.

When you have finished the second full scene, go back and find the Scene Question, the characters' conflicting goals, the answer to the Scene Question and the escalating danger, and note these at the end of the piece.

Then ask yourself: Was the Scene Question clear for the second scene? Was the transition adequate to seamlessly link the two scenes together? Did you choose the right kind of transition, or would another transition technique work better? Did you set up the opening transition into the second scene with an ending "transition alert"? If not, what can you add to incorporate a transition alert?

You have **25 MINUTES** to finish this exercise.

Unit 8: Style/Voice

*"A writer's **voice** is not character alone, it is not style alone; it is far more. A writer's voice—like the stroke of an artist's brush—is the thumbprint of her whole person—her idea, wit, humor, passions, rhythms."*

~Patricia Lee Gauch

EVERY WRITER DREAMS OF developing a unique Voice, a Style that is easily identifiable by readers everywhere. One that is unmistakably their own, inimitable in its essence. Think of Shakespeare, Dickens, Conan-Doyle, Hemingway, Agatha Christie, Elizabeth George, Janet Evanovich, Rosamund Pilcher, Stephen King... A reader could open any of those writers' books and, not even looking at the author's name, know who wrote it simply by the way the story unfolds. By the words and phrases, the sentence structure, the characterizations, the themes and insights.

But what, really, constitutes a writer's Voice? What makes it unique? We all talk (or write) about developing our voice, want to create a special style all our own. But to do that we have to understand what voice and style is, where it comes from, and how we can discover and develop our own. And this isn't simply a matter of going to school or taking writing classes to learn the skills of fiction writing. There's more than skill involved in Voice and Style.

Voice and Style are difficult to define, because they are not just the skills that create them. They are greater than the sum of the elements that go into them. There is an amorphous quality, an indefinable element, that comes only through experience, through self-knowledge, through work, and through trusting your own nature and instincts. The larger part of Voice and Style can be learned. The **most important part** comes from within you, from your very essence.

Voice and Style are made up of a lot of concrete elements that work together to create a separate entity. They're composed of the words a writer chooses and the way those words are put together. The way sentences are structured, the way paragraphs grow, the way scenes develop and connect. A writer's education and life experiences also go into the make-up of Voice and Style. The books a writer reads and the authors a writer tries to emulate play an important role. So does rhythm and pacing, a sense of detail, empathy and sympathy for the human condition, a sense of the absurd, a sense of humor, and a sense of both the profound and the profane. The anecdotes of our lives, our joys and sorrows, and our ability to improvise, to access our own emotional black holes, and to trust that we have important things to say and meaningful themes to explore all become a part of our unique Voice and Style.

Voice and Style, in essence, are us; who we are as human beings, exposed to the world in the words we write, the stories we tell, the emotions we show to the world—and those we choose to hide—the fears and hopes and dreams we tell no one but the characters on the pages of our stories. Voice and Style can be exhilarating, but they can also be terrifying.

One of the nicest compliments I ever received came from a writer friend who was in the middle of reading my latest release, a paranormal suspense novel titled *Proof of Identity*. He told me that he could almost hear my voice as he read, telling him the story of Danae Holloway. He could hear me on the page.

Me. My voice. My Voice. Telling a story as only I can tell it. A story that is the compilation of who I am and what I have done and learned in my life. What more could any writer ask for, than to have a Voice that is uniquely theirs?

The following nine exercises will help you access those parts of your inner self where the essence of *your* Voice resides. They will help you learn to trust your own unique way of telling a story, so you can weave those innate, natural story telling qualities into the skills you can learn in classes: characters, settings, point of view, dialogue, plot, grammar, punctuation, etc. They will help you tap into who you are, so you can begin to hear your own Voice.

Unit 8, Style/Voice: Contents

Lesson #1: Understanding Yourself

OUR STORIES COME FROM within us. They are part of who we are and the way we see and interact with the world. They are informed and created by the truths we discover in our daily lives. Whether you write creative nonfiction or fiction—literary, general, experimental, or any of today's numerous genres—**what you write is you**, put onto paper for the world to see. Clothed in fictional garb, perhaps, but still you.

No one can write your stories because no one experiences life the way you do. No one else thinks the way you do, or draws the same conclusions. If you doubt this, all you have to do is gather a group of writer friends and give each of them the same opening line of a story and let them write on it for 15 minutes.

Not one of them will write the same story that anyone else writes.

I've been teaching classes for over four years now, doing exactly that—giving each of my students the same subject, theme or opening line for the week's exercise—and no one has yet come up with the same treatment. Sometimes two people will choose the same name for a character, or the same occupation, a serendipitous coincidence we find amusing. But the stories are all unique and different, even though they all started with the same first line. Or the same premise/theme.

That's because, even though most of us in the morning group have been together more than four years and have become very close friends, we are still who we are as individuals. No one else has lived my life, or Dennis' life, or Anna's life. No one else has reacted to the events of their life in the same way, made the same decisions, come to the same conclusions, believed—or not—the same things.

When we write from our subconscious—which is the point of timing these exercises (if you haven't yet read the front matter, go back and read "The Value of Timed Writing" on page viii)—we **write from our truth.** We write from the place deep inside where our experiences meet our hearts, where our minds sort through our life and draw conclusions and make decisions. Decisions on what life is. What love is. What pain and struggle means.

The more we know about ourselves—who we were, who we are, and who we are growing to be—the more we can let go and trust the truth of the stories that lie within us. The more we can turn off our conscious mind (until we need it for editing work after the writing is done) and let our life experience inform and guide our words, our characters, our scenes, our themes. For it is there, deep within the truth of who we are and why we are that our Voice resides, the one true Voice that will bring our stories to life for the rest of the world.

READ: *Finding Your Writer's Voice* (Frank & Wall, 1994) page 3-4

Exercise #1: Understanding Yourself*

(Purpose of Exercise: To explore who you are)

WRITE ABOUT WHO YOU are and how you got to be the way you are. Look over your entire life, at all the important and life-changing events that have occurred, and all the people who have been influential. Include your quirks and foibles as well as your talents and your accomplishments.

This is more than a simple biography. It should be a stream-of-consciousness with a philosophical bent, that explores the WHY of you more than the what.

Don't stop to think, just let the words and images flow. Go wherever your instincts take you. Don't stop and don't go back to "correct" words or phrases. Just **put down on paper why you are who you are**. Trust that the deep inner core of yourself will help you learn to see who you really are through the words you put onto the paper.

Set your timer for **15 MINUTES** and start writing.

Lesson #2: Understanding Your Voice

AN EDITOR ONCE ASKED me, "Who do you write like?" I was so startled, I didn't have an answer for her. All I could think was, "I don't write like anyone else. I write like me." I actually felt insulted that she expected me to copycat someone else's writing style.

It took me a while to realize what she was really asking: *What other published author has an audience who would like your books?* But in having to come to terms with what she said as opposed to what she meant, I learned a lot about myself, why I write, and how my Voice grew from the message I needed the world to hear.

A large part of our writing Voice is tied up in the message that is contained in everything we write. It doesn't matter what genre. The message—or theme, if you will—is there, sometimes more obviously than at other times.

I didn't understand this until a writer friend, Debra Davis Hinkle, asked me what the theme was in my writing. I stared at her, dumbfounded. Didn't she know I wrote suspense, paranormal suspense and a sci-fi/fantasy mix? Those are just stories, things I made up to amuse myself and my readers. They didn't have themes, they had plots and puzzles and characters trying to overcome and get what they need to survive. It was "just" genre fiction, escapist literature, not heavy literary work that needed a theme.

I told her all this. She simply blinked at me and said, "Take another look. There's a theme there even if you're not yet aware of it."

Stubborn as I am, I decided to prove her wrong. I went and looked at both my finished stories and those still in progress. Here are a few: *Tangled Webs*, about a woman with partial amnesia; *Proof of Identity*, about a woman who isn't who she thinks she is; *Sins of the Past*, about a woman whose life was built on fiction, not reality (all three published on Amazon) *Piece By Piece*, about a woman with total amnesia; *A Matter of Identity*, about a woman trying to find out who she is (both soon to be released on Amazon and Kindle), *Stealing Shyon*, about a woman trying to come to terms with who she is; *Destany's Daughter*, about a girl who has no idea who she really is (novels in progress; and short stories, "Coffin of Silence," about a woman hiding who she really is; "The Telltale Death," about a man losing sight of who he is; "The SomeWhen Murder," about a woman coming to terms with her abilities; "Figment," about a woman who is invisible; the Skylark investigation series, about a group of women trying to figure out where they and their paranormal abilities fit into life.

Do you see a pattern emerging here? I was shocked when I really started to look. **All my stories are about identity**—finding it, losing it, coming to terms with it, understanding it. And here I thought I was simply writing clever, dark little mysteries and fantasies.

Where does the theme, the message, come from? You. From your life. From what your mind and heart has decided about what you have experienced. From what your mind and heart have decided it means.

My theme relates to the fact that I was adopted at fifteen months old. In one fell swoop I lost the "family" I lived with in the orphanage, my name was changed and my identity, the sense of self I had developed up to that time, vanished. I became someone's daughter and lived with two strangers in an equally strange place. I no longer had a large group of brothers and sisters or any familiar surroundings. I had lost my identity.

And the search for it, for who I really am and why I really am, has become the driving force for my life—and my writing. It forms the base of my Voice, the reason why no one else can write the stories I write in the way I write them. My theme, or message, is stronger now that I am aware of it. Understanding who I am and how I got to be me has helped my Voice to shine through my words like a beacon of hope to the world.

READ: *Finding Your Writer's Voice* (Frank & Wall, 1994) Page 73-76

Exercise #2: Understanding Your Voice*

(Purpose of Exercise: To explore the driving force
behind our writing)

WE ALL HAVE A message hidden (or sometimes not so hidden) in every piece of fiction we write. This message is tied to who we are, the way we see the world around us, how we experience life. It's an integral part of our writer's voice.

Write about the message that's in (or will be in) your fiction work. What are you trying to tell, or want to tell, the reader about life, about the world, about being human? Or, put another way, what are you trying to discover about yourself, or for yourself?

This message (or theme) is the driving force behind your writing. If you think you have more than one message or theme, try to discover the link between them, the commonality that is **the true theme of your voice.**

You have **20 MINUTES** to explore the hidden message that underlies all your work. Start now.

Lesson #3: Voice As Instrument

A WRITER'S VOICE IS not static or or carved in stone. It is dynamic, constantly growing and changing, affected by, and added to, what happens every day. Sometimes a writer's raw voice pours out onto the page, filled with exuberance and emotion. At other times the writing is more restrained, constrained within the parameters of the forms and substance that comprise the rules of grammar and punctuation.

Voice is like a living sculpture that is always being worked on and never quite finished. Or, as Thaisa Frank and Dorothy Walls put it in *Finding Your Writer's Voice*, it can be likened to an orchestra that plays a varied assortment of musical compositions.

In this orchestral Voice, there will be one instrument that stands out from the rest, a main instrument that sets the mood and pace for all the others. This is your raw Voice, the one that pours words onto the paper almost without your conscious awareness. For myself, when that happens I need to go back and read what I have written, for my conscious mind is not fully aware of what my subconscious did. It sometimes feels as though I were merely taking dictation, not creating the words, phrases, sentences and paragraphs myself.

But a story is more than raw Voice poured onto paper. It is the cooperation of a number of elements, all the skills needed to bring the story into life: character, setting, story, plot, dialogue, scenes, style, conflict, subplot, grammar, etc. Each of these is a separate instrument in your writing orchestra, and all work together to produce a harmonious whole.

What instrument is your raw, subconscious Voice? What other instruments chime in to produce chords, runs, harmonies and syncopations? Are all your stories written with the same orchestral configuration? What about the rhythm and pacing? What type of music does your orchestra play when you write? Jazz? Rap? Swing? Classical?

The more we understand the orchestral configuration of our Voice and Style, the more we can trust our Voice to shine through our words. We can let our subconscious take over and give our raw Voice full rein, then bring the other instruments in to add depth and breadth and harmony and syncopation. We can adjust the pacing and rhythm of our word compositions until our readers fall under the spell of the music of our Voice.

READ: *Finding Your Writer's Voice* (Frank & Wall, 1994) Page 77-79

Exercise #3: Voice As Instrument*

(Purpose of Exercise: To explore the nuances of our own voice)

TAKE A FEW MINUTES to think about your writing—the types of things you write, the words you choose, the structure and rhythm of your sentences.

Now compare your writer's voice to an orchestra: where do you belong in the mix of instruments? Is your raw voice a woodwind, a string or a brass instrument? Is it a piccolo, a flute, a horn, a cello, a violin, a piano or a bass? Do you find places to use percussion instruments in your writer's voice?

Tell what main instrument your raw voice is, and what other instruments you add in completing your writer's composition. What genre of music do you write with your voice—Classical, Country & Western, Rock, Easy Listening? Jazz, Reggae, Rap? Something else? Are all your works written to the same configuration of instruments, or do the instruments change places depending on the piece you are writing?

Give yourself **15 MINUTES** to write about your writing instrument, your voice, as an orchestral composition. Set your timer now and begin.

Lesson #4: What Drives the Story?

WHAT ACTIVATES YOUR VOICE? What inspires you to put pen to paper? What makes a simple event—a woman driving down the street with her dress sticking out of the car door—turn into a trigger that begins the story process in your mind? Understanding what motivates you to craft a story is key to working with your voice.

Perhaps the above example does nothing for your creativity until you wonder where she is driving from, where she is driving to, and why. What is the solution to the puzzle? Or you wonder why she didn't care enough to make sure her dress was fully inside the car before closing the door. Is she sad, scared, alone, mourning? Or maybe too excited about the future to worry about the now. Then again, it could be the symbolism of that scrap of material jutting from the car door that intrigues you and begins the story process. What does that piece of fabric mean?

Stories are driven in **three main ways**, and our voice is attuned to one more than the others. Knowing what triggers our voice to sit up and take notice, which of the driving forces captures our attention, helps us to understand our voice better and work with it more effectively.

Stories are either:

    1. **Plot** driven,

    2. **Character** driven, or

    3. **Vision** driven.

In plot driven stories, the plot is the most important element. Everything hinges on the events that happen, on the puzzle and solving it. The characters are secondary to the plot. Most mysteries and thrillers are plot driven stories because of their very nature, the puzzle that must be solved. Think of Ken Follett, Agatha Christie, Conan-Doyle—plot commands the place of honor. Although there are some exceptions to mysteries being plot driven, Elizabeth George being one of them. The mysteries in her stories are plot driven, but the stories themselves revolve around the characters and are character driven.

Characters are uppermost in character driven stories. Who they are, how their lives intersect, what they learn and how they grow and change—this takes the place of importance. All the events that happen do so to advance the growth of the characters.

Vision driven stories are all the rest, those that are based on ideas, images, tone/point of view, or language. They are more abstract than the other two, a philosophical treatise on the meaning of life itself. Both plot and character are secondary to the exploration of the idea, image, tone or language—the vision of the writer—itself. Literary and exploratory fiction are usually vision driven stories.

These are general categories into which most finished stories will fit. But that doesn't mean that they began the way they ended up. Take the example of the woman driving down the street. You first become intrigued by who she is, why she was so careless with her dress, and in the writing discover the plot of a mystery taking over. Or your voice may be triggered by the symbolism inherent in the scrap of fabric visible outside the car door, but you find the character's development becomes the driving force of the story as you write.

What triggers, or activates, your voice isn't necessarily what begins the story, either. It can be something that happens at the end, or somewhere in the middle. It can be something a character says even before the story begins, or long after it has ended. You may start writing in the middle and work both ways. You might start at the end and work backwards.

The important thing is to understand which driving force makes your creative voice sit up and take notice. The point is to **recognize what gets you started** on the story-making process, not where the material ends up in the story, or even which category the finished story fits into.

Look for what excites you. What makes you say, "What if?" What makes you daydream? What makes characters knock on your head, demanding to be let loose? Give your voice free rein to work. Pay attention to what makes you want to start a story. Don't feel you have to write a plot driven thriller like Tess Gerritsen or a vision driven book like Joyce Carol Oates just because you admire their work. **Write what excites you**, what feels compelling, enticing, urgent. Write what comes naturally to you.

READ: *Finding Your Writer's Voice* (Frank & Wall, 1994) Page 85-89

Exercise #4: What Drives the Story?*

(Purpose of Exercise: To explore the driving force of our writing)

CONSIDER THE LAST THREE fiction pieces you have written. (If you haven't finished anything yet, use the pieces you're working on or considering starting.) Analyze them as to whether they are **character**, **plot** or **vision** driven. Then tell **why** you chose that driving force.

Now, take one of the stories and change its driving force: i.e., if it is plot driven, make it character or vision driven. If it is character driven, make it plot or vision driven. And so forth.

What would have to change for it to have a different driving force? Would it be the same story? Do you think your writer's voice would also change to accommodate the new driving force of the story? Why or why not?

Give yourself **20 MINUTES** to finish this exercise, starting now.

Lesson #5: Know thyself—Voice

IMITATION MAY BE THE sincerest form of flattery, but in writing the only true value you gain from imitating other writers is to help you take risks and get out of your comfort zone. Writers don't write in a vacuum, for all that writing is a solitary occupation. Writing in another writer's style helps you experiment, find what fits, understand how to change and alter that style to how you would do it—in short, to play with the limitations of your own voice.

But in the end, **you only have yourself to work with**. You may be able to brilliantly imitate your favorite author, say Elizabeth George, but there will be nothing of either you or her in the story. The heart, the soul, the excitement will be missing, because you are not Elizabeth George, and only she can put herself into the writing.

Finding your own voice and style means you have to accept that you have only your own ordinary, unique life to work with. And you have to accept the fact that what to you may be dull and uninteresting may fill readers with awe. Working with your voice takes trust. And courage.

Courage? you ask. What courage? It's just a bunch of words on a piece of paper, virtual or not. What's courage got to do with it?

No, it's not just words. It's you, too. Because those words are filtered through your mind, your emotions, your life. They pick up **your essence**. When your work is infused with your true voice, you are present in that work in a very real way.

When we read a book that intrigues us, that takes us into an imaginary world and doesn't let go until the very end, we come away knowing not only the world and its characters, but also the author. We feel that we have "met" him, perhaps over dinner, walked with him in the park, learned about who she is, what she likes and dislikes. Because the writer leaves a piece of him- or herself on the pages of the book, we have not just read a good story but but also met a new friend—the author.

We can't help this. Our voice is so tied up with who we are, so intrinsically a part of our essence, that it spills out into everything we write. We bare our souls, reveal intimacies, expose our imagination, our vision, our quirks and our personalities **even if we never write a biographical word**. We become intimate strangers with those who read our stories. As Frank and Walls say, "Writing is an inevitably and effortlessly self-revealing act."

That is why it takes courage to be a writer with a strong, solid voice. It's not for the faint of heart. And it takes curiosity, the ability to accept yourself for who you are, and the ability to detach from your own life and look at it through a writer's eyes, and then reattach and use what you have seen and learned about yourself in your work.

READ: *Finding Your Writer's Voice* (Frank & Wall, 1994) Page 54-57

*Exercise #5: Know thyself—Voice**

(Purpose of Exercise: To explore who we are as writers and people)

A CONSISTENT VOICE COMES from self-knowledge. One the best ways to know yourself is to see yourself through the eyes of another person.

An alien from another planet comes to Earth and meets you, a famous author. You spend a weekend together getting to know each other. During this time, you show a trait or quality of yours that you don't particularly like—**a real one**, not a made up one.

Now, become the alien character and write a letter to someone back on your home planet. Tell about the writer you just met, letting the negative quality or trait dominate your description. Find humor and/or absurdity in this trait or quality.

Set your timer for **20 MINUTES** and begin writing.

Lesson #6: Sorting Your Inner Cacophony

AS A WRITER, YOU will probably hear many voices inside your head. These are all aspects of your voice, speaking to you, clamoring for notice. Some will be mysterious phrases that don't seem to connect to anything (*caramel custard cupcakes; never again, baby*) Others may form questions that lead to story ideas (*What if a kid loses his socks at school?*). Some may be characters speaking to you (*I never should have eaten that last donut*). Still others may even seem to start a story (*Only the good die young, but Anders wasn't young. And he wasn't good, either. So why was he dead?*)

No, you're not going crazy, you're a writer. Words are a writer's stock in trade, and our writer's voice is constantly throwing words at us, urging us to sit down and begin to write. Our subconscious mind notices everything, hears everything, and sinks it all into a "subconscious soup" from which our voice pulls selections at random.

Think of your subconscious as a huge fallow field. Everything that happens to us, everything we see, hear, think and experience, gets plowed under in that field. Eventually seeds sprout and our voice picks the stems—flowers and weeds both—and presents the bouquet to our minds.

Our job is to take the bunch of flowers and weeds and play with it. Explore the story ideas (see *Workbook #3: Unit 5, Plot* for exercises), let the characters reveal themselves (see *Workbook #1: Unit 1, Character* for exercises) and play with the random words and phrases (see *Workbook #1: Unit 3, Story* for exercises) that pop up. Some ideas will fizzle almost immediately. Some will take you on a longer journey before vanishing. And some will come to fruition in a full story or book.

Keep a notebook and jot down the cacophony as it spills out from your mind. Don't censor any of it. You never know when a random phrase, character or idea will spark exactly what you need for your next story. Some of the creatures you release from this Pandora's Box of Voice might be scary, wild and wonderful. Give them all full rein, become their scribe and enjoy the journey into your own creativity.

Don't cut off the voices too quickly or you could miss the potential in them. Let your subconscious play for a while and set your conscious mind, the one that criticizes and scoffs, on the sidelines for the duration. You're only playing here, not creating Nobel Prize-winning literature, so give your critic the day off. Learn to listen to your inner cacophony and recognize its value. Keep asking, what can I get from this situation, this person, this image?

READ: Finding Your Writer's Voice (Frank & Wall, 1994) Page 38-39

Exercise #6: Sorting Your Inner Cacophony*

(Purpose of Exercise: To explore the voices inside your head)

SIT QUIETLY AND LISTEN to the myriad voices inside you. Then jot down 5 to 10 things these different voices say.

It could be whole sentences, a single sentence or just a phrase, an observation, a description of something, a name, etc. They could be voices from characters you've created in stories you are working on who haven't appeared yet, characters from stories you've thought about but haven't started yet, or just random characters that people your psyche who haven't yet found a story home.

Now, pick one of the voices you put down on paper and from what you wrote describe the character. What does this person look like? Sound like? Think like? Male or female? Young or old? What style and colors of clothing does he/she like? What kind of car does he/she drive? What is that person's favorite food? Color? Song? Movie? Is this character human, animal, alien? Keep writing for the allotted time.

Take **15 MINUTES** to finish this exercise.

Lesson #7: Distillation

THERE ARE TWO KINDS of voice in any piece of writing. The voice of the narrator, be it a narrating character or a narrator separate from the characters. That kind of voice, the story voice, is addressed at length in ***Workbook #1: Character, Setting, Story***.

The voice I'm talking about here is the other voice, the one we've been working on in this unit, the writer's voice. Your voice.

Yes, each of your characters has his or her own voice within the story. But the piece as a whole also has its own voice. Think of it this way. A story features a character, Natalie, who is saucy and irreverent. Natalie's a bit of a wise-ass, always has a smart comeback even if it gets her in trouble. She suffers from speak-before-you-think syndrome.

Now put her in an office where there's an overbearing boss and three men who want to date her even though two of them are married. And ask Elizabeth George, Bob Mayer, Dean Koontz and Janet Evanovich to each write Natalie's story, with Natalie as the narrating character.

Natalie's voice as she relates her story will be similar in all four versions, because she is who she is: a wise-ass smart mouth who can't help but have a skewed view of her world. But the overall voice of the story itself—the words chosen, the way the words are put together, what is important and what is left out—will be completely different, because the authors are different people. One will feel more literary, one very intense. One will come across as humorous and another spare and tight in its prose.

Four different writers, writing about the same kind of character, with four different voices.

Voice, as we have discussed, comes from a combination of the skills you master as you learn to write, and who you are, the essence of yourself that you instill into your work. All writers know that feeling when the words just come, effortlessly, pouring forth like a fountain. You almost have to go back when you are finished and re-read to see what has happened in the story. It seems as though the characters have taken over and you have merely been taking dictation.

When that happens, you find places that seem to sing. The words dance off the page, imbued with a life of their own. These are the places where your inborn voice shines through. These are the places where writing is a joy, not a task to be completed. These are the places where you are writing from your heart, your soul.

Do you know what your own voice sounds like? Can you recognize yourself on the page, and identify those places where you are less present, where you perhaps slip into the style and voice of that historical romance you've been reading late at night, or the amazing otherworldly series that's got you hooked? Do you know what your raw voice sounds like?

It's imperative for every writer to know his/her own voice, to understand what makes their heart sing. To know that when the prose gets pared down to is bare essence your message comes through clearly. Or when the mystery becomes lyrical your essence is painted on the page. Or when readers laugh out loud, they laugh in delight with you, the author. When we know what our voice truly is, and have experienced its unique specialness, it is easier to trust it to lead our stories to where they need to go.

READ: *Write Away* (George, 2004) Page 19, first paragraph; page 195-197; *Finding Your Writer's Voice* (Frank & Wall, 1994) Page 24

*Exercise #7: Distillation**

(Purpose of Exercise: To distill your voice down to
its essential components)

THIS EXERCISE WILL TAKE you a few weeks to complete, though it will take **only 10 MINUTES A DAY** on the days you will actually write. It will be tempting not to bother with it, but if you do it, you will find out amazing things about yourself, your writing style and your unique voice.

Starting today, write for **10 MINUTES A DAY FOR 7 DAYS**. For example, if you begin this exercise on a Wednesday, you will write for 10 minutes today, and on Thursday, Friday, Saturday, Sunday, Monday and Tuesday. Write at top speed, anything that comes into your head. Don't stop to think, just keep writing as fast as you can.

Each day can be a separate piece, or you can start each day where you left off the day before. Or any combination. The only caveat is that **you cannot go back and re-read anything** you've written. Once you finish, it is done. DO NOT read anything after it's been written. Write for 10 minutes only and stop.

Then, the day after after the last 10-minute writing session (as in the example, the last session was on Tuesday, so do this on Wednesday), **put the writings away unread for 1 week**. Then, the following Wednesday, get out what you wrote and read it out loud. Highlight or underline passages, phrases and words that leap out at you, that grab your attention.

Now, begin the 10 minute sessions again, each time starting with one of the marked passages, phrases or words, chosen randomly. Write for 7 days (Wednesday through Tuesday), **always starting with a new marked word or phrase**. Do **not** continue from where you left off this time. Let each day be a new piece, started with a new marked phrase or word. And like last time, **do not go back and re-read** anything you have written. Write full out for **10 MINUTES EACH TIME**, then stop and put the writing away, unread. Start this on Wednesday and continue for 6 more days (Wednesday through Tuesday).

Now put all the writings away for another week. Then take them out and read aloud the second batch of writing. Again highlight or underline everything that stands out, those parts that are unusual, provocative and/or challenging.

Now, **delete everything you haven't marked**. Read what remains aloud. You may end up with a prose poem, a surprising non-sequitur with its own sense of wholeness, a surreal story or humorous nonsense. This is the essence of your voice.

For clarity, here's a daily listing of the process. If Week #1 begins on a Wednesday, as in the example:

Week 1: Write for 10 minutes on Wednesday, Thursday, Friday, Saturday, Sunday, Monday, Tuesday.

Week 2: On Wednesday, put the writing away for 1 week.

Week 3: On the following Wednesday, read, highlight and start writing for 10 minutes on Wednesday, Thursday, Friday, Saturday, Sunday, Monday, Tuesday, starting each day with a new highlighted phrase or part.

Week 4: On Wednesday, put the writing away for 1 week.

Week 5: On the following Wednesday, highlight what jumps out at you and delete everything else.

Lesson #8: Voice and Style

A WRITER'S STYLE, AS opposed to his voice, is a compilation of the techniques (or writing tools) he's learned, the proficiency with which he uses them, and his own personality. Style is something that can only be partially learned. The rest comes from experience, practice and the fire inside that makes one sit down and put words on paper.

Some writers have a very terse style, like the way Hemingway wrote: words scraped down to the bare minimum. Other writers glory in words and mix a literary or even lyrical quality into their work, as does Elizabeth George. Others infuse humor, irony, naiveté, mystery, the arcane, philosophy, and so on, into what they write. They can't help it. It's part of who they are, the way they see the world and humanity's place in it.

The way we put words onto paper tells a lot about us, the writer. Our writing style gives readers a glimpse into our lives and our minds. It helps them "see" us, makes them feel as though they know us. It creates a bond between reader and writer, one that if we are not careful we can easily break. Staying true to our style is one way to keep that bond strong.

But to stay true to our style, we need to know what it is. We need to understand how we write, what the choice of words and how we use them tell readers about us beyond the limitations of the story. How does the way we write reflect who we are? When we know that, we can understand and accept the uniqueness that our writing style reveals, and stop wishing we wrote like someone else.

But make no mistake. Writing is a **dynamic art**, and our writing style will continue to grow and develop as the years pass. The more we learn of writing techniques, the more refined our style will become. The more we experience in life, the deeper our style will grow. While the basic style may remain the same, the nuances of it will broaden and reach out further with each piece we write, each day that passes.

It is a journey into growth that we undertake every time we pick up a pen (or put fingers on the keyboard), not a journey to a final destination. Writers never "arrive." We are always in process, on our way. Growing and developing all along the way. The following exercise is a good one to do periodically, maybe once a year or so, to help you mark your progress on your writing journey and pinpoint the growth along the way. Remember: the more you know about yourself, the better a writer you will be.

*Exercise #8: Voice and Style**

(Purpose of Exercise: To define and delineate your personal style)

THINK ABOUT STYLE AS applied to writing, your own personal style. Write out a definition of your writing style, including these areas:

technique; philosophy; themes explored; personality. Then answer, in length, the following question.

What would someone else have to know about you in order to write in the same style?

Set your timer for **20 MINUTES** and begin now.

Lesson #9: Know Thyself—Style

BEING A WRITER TAKES commitment. "Yes, I know," you say. Everyone knows a novel doesn't get written in a day. Nor do most short stories. It takes time to learn, to write and then to rewrite. Lots of hours at the computer, using what Elizabeth George, via Australia's Bryce Courtenay, author of *The Power of One*, calls bum glue: Gluing one's butt to the chair seat until the book is finished.

But there's more than just commitment to writing and the time it takes. There's also doing and/or acquiring what you know you need to succeed: A quiet place to write; time for yourself on deserted beach once a week; travel to cities where you want to place your stories; computer expertise; a writing partner; a more comfortable chair, a writing partner or critique group... Whatever it may be.

We live in a world of distractions. We can't walk into a restaurant or a store without being bombarded by music, advertising posters, flashing lights, etc. Cell phones have made private time a thing of the past. We can watch television and even movies on our computers, tablets and even smart phones.

And there are our obligations: Money to earn, bills to pay, children to raise, families to care for, friends who need us, food to shop for and prepare, clothing to purchase, vehicles to service, houses to clean, yards to groom, laundry to do, etc. There is always something that seems more immediate, more important, than sitting on a chair writing about something that isn't "real."

It's way too easy to allow life to get in the way of what we need to fulfill ourselves. And with our busy schedules, it's often close to impossible to carve out even a few minutes a week to do what we want to do, much less be able to pinpoint what it is we do need to be a successful writer (however we choose to define success to ourselves).

But part of our writing style develops from the confidence of knowing who we are as writers, and taking care of the writer part of us. It's knowing what we need, assessing our ability to get what we need, and then taking steps to make sure it happens. Having a clear goal in mind, and knowing the steps we need to take to achieve that goal, allows us to write with authority and confidence. Because we don't have a sense of failure pressing down on us. We aren't laboring under a false sense of "This won't come to anything anyway." Or, "I can't do this." Or "I don't know where I'm going." Or even, "I don't deserve this."

All those thoughts are killers. They kill our trust. They kill our confidence. They kill our ability to let go and simply write. They drain away our ability to conceive characters, to plot stories, to arrange words on paper that will enthrall readers. They keep us from taking the next step, and the next, and the next. And we end up procrastinating instead of writing. Mowing the lawn instead of outlining the next chapter. Cleaning the house instead of taking that writing class. Reading a bag full of books instead of writing our own.

Know that you were born to write, to be a writer. That is why you have this workbook in your hands. That is why your head is full of characters, settings and situations that at times feel more real than your own life. Know that **you deserve to write**, to feel the success of a finished product in your hands. Then do the following exercise and begin to take the steps needed for you to fulfill your writing dreams. Set your style truly free by crafting a game plan to follow, step-by-step.

Exercise #9: Know Thyself—Style*
(Purpose of Exercise: To understand your motivations
and the blockages to attaining your goals)

WRITE OUT A LIST of what you need to nourish yourself as a writer, things you don't have now. What are the conditions you **need** to consider yourself a successful working writer (whether or not you are selling/publishing your work)? What are the most important things (i.e., time, a place to work, uninterrupted peace, etc.)? Put everything on the list, all the big and little stuff. Don't leave anything out, but do leave a few lines between each item on the list.

Now go back and, in those blank lines, write down what is **stopping** you from having those things. Be sure to put down all the big things and the little things.

Put a star in front of the **top 5 most important items** on your "Need It" list. Look at what is stopping you from getting them. What can't you change? Now look at what you can change to help yourself get what you need to fully nourish yourself as a writer.

Make a "to do" list of those actions you can take to begin recreating your life so there is ample time for your writing and for the things that nourish your writing life. If applicable, note down the timeline involved in those actions. Pledge to yourself (and to your writing group if you have one, or email your list to me) that you will have a specific set of actions completed by a specific date. Make a check list that you can check off as you accomplish each goal.

Give yourself **45 MINUTES** to finish this exercise and make your checklist, then pin the list up where you can review it every day and renew your pledge to yourself to accomplish those goals within the allotted time frame.

Examples From My Class Writing

THESE ARE EXAMPLES OF writings I do in my workshops along with my students as I teach each lesson. Please bear in mind that they are done in the 15-20 minute sessions and have not been edited or corrected.

Lesson #1: Understanding Yourself

I am someone who never fits in, even when I make my own place. I'm never comfortable whether alone or in a crowd. I believe the reason for that goes back to my childhood, to the first months after my birth.

I was adopted at 15 months of age. Yes, old for an adoptee; most parents-to-be want infants, so they can bond with them completely, learn who their little person is from almost day one. A tabula rasa, as it were. There would be pictures of growth, milestones in the life of this newly developing personality: first crawl, first step, first tooth, first haircut. Photos of themselves cradled in loving arms, safe and protected and loved.

But I grew up without any early pictures. No record of my first 15 months of life. I was adopted, and not as an infant, but as a toddler with her personality set. I grew up believing that no one wanted me, not until these two really gullible people came along and the people at the adoption agency could foist me on them and finally rid themselves of the burden I caused for them.

We didn't mesh well from the start, my mother and I. I was too stubborn, too loud, too demanding, too much my own person. And I was suffering the loss of what for me had been my family, all the other kids in the orphanage where I was raised those 15 months. I like to say, only half-joking (even though only older people understand the reference these days) that Mom wanted Shirley Temple but she got Jane Withers.

Only half-joking because sometimes—most times—I feel like the characters Jane Withers portrayed. Never good enough, always wanting and always found wanting no matter how hard I try. I know now, as an adult, that these feelings are not true, are in fact based on inadequate information. They are based on decisions and conclusions I made on an unconscious level before I even knew how to talk. But I think that makes them even more powerful.

I came to understand as I grew up that I was smarter and more intuitive than most of my classmates. And even than most of the adults around me. And I was often taken to task for the insights I discovered, because they were unseemly in a child of seven or ten or thirteen. Somehow in my long-go past I made the decision to simply be who I was, to not play a game I had no chance of winning. I spent long years in grade school trying to be just like everyone else, only to be foiled at every turn—because I was not like everyone else, and nothing I could do could change who I was. An outsider. Someone who didn't belong.

There wasn't anything specific that anyone did to make me feel this way. The kids were simply kids, acting like kids, unaware of the sensitivities around them. By high school I decided to flaunt my 'otherness,' to be a true rebel without a cause. I allowed my mind free rein to grow and develop, refusing to dumb down in order to fit in. And I think, in retrospect, that I garnered a portion of respect from my classmates, even if I wasn't aware of it at the time. Secretly I still wanted to belong.

I wanted so much, knew I was capable of so much, when I entered college and then graduated, but fear of not being good enough kept me from stepping out and fully exploring myself. I feared success more than I feared failure. At least failure I was familiar with, having practiced it so often. I opted out of trying by getting married and never testing my wings.

But now, at this late stage in my life, alone and on my own, I am finding my base, the place where I belong, where I can actually dream and accomplish. I am beginning finally to believe in myself and my abilities, to trust that it is not a fluke, that I am a good writer and a really great teacher/mentor/editor. That I am funny and interesting—at least when it comes to writing—and have important things to say. I wonder sometimes where I would be right now, who I would be, had I believed in myself sooner. Had I had a full life ahead of me once I trusted in my talent, instead of only a few years. Still, I'm grateful for what I do have, for what I am accomplishing and will still accomplish. Life is good; it's fun and interesting and exhilarating. I've found my place, at least in the writing community. I'm still searching for the rest.

Exercise #2: Understanding Your Voice

In my writing I explore the theme of belonging: who a person is in the world. It goes back to my own need to discover who I am. I have no idea who my birth parents are, although I know a little bit, the amount that my adoptive parents discovered before they adopted me. The agency couldn't tell them anything about my origins and they wanted to be sure my adoptive parents really wanted me. So, when the social worker left the room, on the pretext of getting coffee, she left my file open on the desk, sure my parents would look at it. They did. They discovered my birth mother's name and her ethnicity, my original name, the fact that she was a college art student and my father was an older man, an architect, who was not married. I don't know why they didn't marry, don't know if he ever knew of my existence. But I do know (my parents told me all this when I was an adult, when my son was 15 months old) that my birth mother tried to keep me. I wasn't released for adoption until I was 15 months old. I have no memory of her visiting me, but then I was too young to be cognizant of such things at the time.

I've always wondered how I got to be conceived—not physically, that is obvious, but the why. What was their relationship, my birth parents? Were they in love, or was he a visiting teacher who took advantage of her and then left town? Do I have relatives somewhere in this world, half-brothers and sisters who could fill the empty spaces in my psyche? And if what the Ancient Wisdom Cosmology says is true, that we choose our lives, choose the main events in order to learn lessons, what is the lesson I am supposed to learn here? Why would I agree to a life of such yearning and emptiness that can never be truly filled?

This is what I explore in my stories. My main characters are misfits in society in some way, struggling to understand who they are and what that means, how they can find a full and fulfilled life. I use various devices, from full and partial amnesia to hard-headed outspokenness and comedy, to psychic gifts that separate my characters from the average person. Then I put them in situations that force them to confront who they are in order to survive. Understanding who they are is the only way to survive, because that understanding holds the key to the strategies that will keep them safe.

And though I know that my writing explores vicariously what I want to know—who I am and why I am—I'm also hoping that there are many people out there who can also be helped in their search for belonging. In understanding of self. In finding a fulfilling life. Then we all will have a place to belong.

Exercise #3: Voice As Instrument

Story: *Proof of Identity*, a novel of paranormal suspense (published 2014)
Main Instrument: Violin

As a violin I am able to sustain both quiet times and periods of deep intensity. The violin touches the heart, pulls the emotions to the fore, makes listeners combine with the music and feel things they perhaps have not felt—or let themselves feel—for a long time. Like a slowly rising tide, the violin can gently float listeners toward a distant place, enmeshing them in a tide that, once it has hold of someone, will not let that person go.

As violin, I can sustain the peak of tension and suspense, drawing it out until nerves fray and limbs tremble. And as violin, I can also sink to the depths, evoking mystery, magic and despair. Completely versatile, violin can be playful when needed, even arch and sophisticated.

For support and emphasis, bassoon reverberates beneath many of the darker scenes, adding the thud of a quickening heartbeat and the aura of doom to the lighter strains of violin. Bass also adds its clear depth to the mix, emphasizing bassoon's heartbeat. Kettle drum intrudes, bringing in a strain of evil that colors future musical interludes.

The subtle plays of violin, bassoon and bass allow me the freedom to create atmosphere and explore character in a suspense story that traditionally is plot-driven, because I rarely use plot as a driving device for my stories.

Had this story been written by horn, it would be less deep, have less protracted sieges of mystery and magic. It would shout rather than whisper, though at times horn can also lower its voice as necessary. But the deep richness of bassoon and bass would be overshadowed by the ego of horn. The story would no longer be suspense, but would slip into the thriller genre, a fast, plot-driven genre.

Voice as Instrument in General

I feel that my main voice is a piano, a Steinway Grand. My pacing and rhythms follow the glissandos of classical music and for me, classical music means a piano, even though a multitude of other instruments are used, especially violin. The piano can be dark and deadly, or light and airy; terrifying in intensity or soft and romantic. And I feel my writing uses all those elements in my stories. There is always a romantic undertone in my stories, although not prominent enough to shift into actual romance genre. The piano can carry the main theme of the music only being played one note at a time, or it can carry the entire weight of the story in its chords and runs.

I also use a deep base as counterpoint to the danger in my stories, a relentless throb that ratchets up tension to the breaking point. Violins also play a large part, adding fullness to the background stories and daily lives of my characters. I love adding percussions to the story to enhance specific moments or call the reader's attention to a subtle clue dropped into an otherwise still pond. French horns add a piquant air at times when close friends share special moments with each other, and lately—at least in one story—a piccolo intrudes on the deep, darkness of the piano and base to add comic relief. My endings almost always include the harp, presaging hope for the future, even if that future is still a long way off. There is a definite lack of brass in my orchestra, though horns do make momentary appearances at times of high drama.

Lesson #4: What Drives the Story?

Stories Analyzed: "The Cabdriver"; *A Matter of Identity*; "The Collector"; *Proof of Identity; Tangled Webs*

My stories are mostly character-driven. Though it usually is a situation that intrigues me, that pulls my initial interest, it is the people affected by those situations that keeps my interest high. I love to explore how different people react to circumstances beyond their control, and explore the psychological ramifications of their actions and decisions. Though plot is important in most of my work because I write suspense—which is plot-driven genre—the way I choose to develop my stories hinges more on the characters involved than what is happening. The plot unfolds almost by itself, but I'm never quite sure what my characters will do. Because of that, I do not—cannot—outline more than a chapter or two. The first time I outlined four chapters, by the time I reached the beginning of the third chapter the story had gone in a totally different direction and I had to scrap the outline. Even though the main plot points remained the same—what had to happen still happened—the way the characters reacted and tried to take control of their lives twisted the story in directions I had never consciously thought about.

If I took any of my stories and made them fully plot-driven, they would no longer be as vital or rich. Readers would lose their connection to the people in the story. While they might still feel for the characters, they would be more aware of what is happening and less of who it is happening to, and therefore more interested in seeing where the story is going, rather than in the effect events are having on the characters. That is the reason I don't truly care for thrillers: they are so plot-driven that I can't wallow in the characters and relationships despite the suspenseful plot; I don't see or live vicariously their lives beyond the main story plot.

I don't think I could write a fully plot-driven piece, unless it was very short. I could write a vision-driven story, because for me the vision or idea or theme would be closely aligned to character. An interesting experiment for me, I think, would be to write a story that didn't have human characters in it, a story of the elements, or an abstraction that did not touch people. And now I've got an idea for yet another tale to add to my story queue!

Story Analyzed: Suspense novel *Piece By Piece*: driven by one woman's quest to discover who she is. The plot, although a mystery, is merely a device to help her discover the answers she needs.

If I took *Piece By Piece* and turned it into a plot-driven story, it would change drastically. The main character, Julie, would stay the same, but the other main character, the man, would have to be someone else. Probably a police detective, or a private eye. There would be more police-procedural type of scenes, more investigation, more emphasis on what is happening rather than why. The main focus of the story would be the investigation of why Julie is being pursued, rather than discovering who she is, and who the people are who are chasing her. The most important factor would be why the bad guys want her dead, not how she is to survive or what her true identity is. Finding out who she is would only matter because it would shed light on the what and why.

My writing would have to be leaner, contain much less of the interpersonal relationships that make up the main emphasis of the story now. It would have less emotion, more factual investigation, and perhaps even the main factor in Julie's life, her amnesia, would be scrapped in favor of the plot being more police investigation oriented. It would cease being a suspense story and become more a classic mystery.

Lesson #5: Know thyself—Voice

Letter Home From an Alien Visitor:

Digita,

Hey, how's it going? I've been here on Terra only two weeks and already I'm so homesick. You wouldn't believe these creatures—human beings, that's what they call themselves, "be"-ings, like they have to keep reminding themselves they're alive and sentient. Although sentient is a matter for discussion, in my opinion. You ask me, they rarely let themselves just be. They're too busy doing, all the time on the go. Kraka forbid they ever just sit and look within themselves, for all they yak on and on about self-enlightenment and spirituality.

Oh, and you won't believe who I met last night! You remember that book on writing we read just before I left? The one that lays it all out: how to start, where to get ideas, first draft, second, revise and so on? Yes, that's right. Susan Tuttle herself, in the flesh (though a whole lot older than that picture on the back cover. Who does she think she's kidding, anyway?) I actually got to sit down and talk to her for a while—it was so worth the extra apppleduns it cost for this side excursion. I couldn't believe an author I knew was in the room, much less that I got to talk to her! Let me tell you, did I learn a lot about writers from her.

I thought, after reading that book of hers, that she would be this really sophisticated, confident, articulate person who would dazzle me with the way she organizes her writing schedule to fit everything in. Boy, was I wrong! She just sat there like a bump on a log, looking like she wished she were somewhere else, giving me nervous smiles and saying, 'Gosh, I don't know," a lot. And when I asked her how many words a day she wrote, she looked at me like I was crazy, and said, "I don't write every day. Actually, I don't write unless I have to. I don't even get any ideas until the deadline is just about passed. Then I write like crazy to make up for lost time."

"But what about drafts? Revisions? Editing?" I asked, scarcely able to believe my ears.

"Drafts?" She gave me a confused stare. "I don't do drafts. I just write and out it comes and I send it in and that's that. There's no time for drafts or revisions."

"But you put it in your book. The one on writing. First draft, second, then revisions and stuff. What about all that?"

"Well, to tell you the truth, I had to think of something to write and that seemed to be the accepted party line. I'd left it too late to think of anything else, so…" she shrugged. "Besides, no one would believe that's the way I do it. See, I'm always late. For everything. I'll be late for my own funeral, I swear. Maybe I just like working under pressure. Or maybe I just don't like working at all." She shrugged again. "Who knows? Who are you, again? I'm terrible with names. But I love that purple and blue hair/

fur/shag thing you've got going on top of your head. Mind if I use it in my next novel? It's due in two weeks and I still don't have my characters down…I'll probably be late for this deadline, too."

Honestly, Digita, I was flabbergasted. Appalled. And enchanted. And, like Tuttle, I'm late for dinner. Write to you again, soon! Miss you!
Your friend,
Elgarned

Lesson #6: Sorting Your Inner Cacophony

Voices inside my head:

It shouldn't have happened.

Help me! Oh, God, help me!

The winding way of Carabasa

Once upon a time nothing at all happened. Deity saw it, and it was good.

Jerrilynn stood at the threshold of her life and wished she could go back.

Anders looked at the knife and wondered if he could cut that unending song out of his brain.

Pick one voice: Anders

Anders is forty-seven, married with 4 grown children, though his oldest son, who got downsized a year go, is threatening to move back home with his wife and twin infants. He never loved his wife, married her because she got pregnant, and has resented the responsibilities of fatherhood and marriage that have kept him from realizing his dream: to operate a hot-air balloon tours business. He works as the night manager of the local outlet of a national chain grocery store.

He has a soft, deep basso-profundo voice that seems to rumble from deep in his broad chest. His friends want him to apply for a job reading for an online enterprise that showcases local writers' works. But Anders is too shy to even consider doing such a thing, even though he would be hidden from view. But having his voice out for public consumption feels to Anders as though he would be losing a part of himself. The listening public, like a gigantic succubus, would drain the life from him with their ears.

Anders is filled with trepidation and superstition. Step-on-a-crack and salt-over-the-shoulder rule his days and nights. He wears dark and drab colors—maroon, olive, charcoal and black—and favors polo shirts and denim. He wears boat shoes without socks year-round, his one affectation of sophistication. He stands about 5'11" in his stocking feet and weighs in at 205. His body is heavily muscled and stocky, with rounded shoulders and what his sister once told him were "thunder thighs." His eyes are an odd shade of turquoise and his hair, which he wears long enough to pull back in a pigtail, is a thick and lustrous auburn. High cheekbones and a square jaw hint at native American genes somewhere in his makeup. He drives a Subaru sedan that's about 10 years old, dark maroon, but in his imagination pilots a classic 57 Chevy in canary yellow with red and orange flames racing down its sides.

He rarely reads anything but golf magazines, even though he doesn't play the game. He tried it once or twice, but was bored out of his mind by the third hole. Still, he wonders what he missed, since so many men—and women, too—seem to thrive on the inane quiet of chasing a ball around artificially manicured lawns. Which is why he reads the magazines, searching for what passed him by on the links.

He watches old sitcom reruns on TV while perusing the newspaper and noting stock prices in case he ever has any extra money to invest. He never does. He spends a lot of time alone, has only a few acquaintances and no close friends. He makes elaborate wood birdhouses in his basement workshop, which he donates to local charities to sell, his way of helping those less fortunate than he is, though he doesn't feel the least bit fortunate.

If he could, he would eat Chinese food every day, especially egg drop soup. He listens to easy listening tunes on the radio in the car, but somehow the station got changed and an ABBA song has been echoing non-stop in his head for the past three weeks. He can even hear it in his dreams. Which is why he is staring at a knife display in the sporting good section of Wal-Mart instead of finalizing the bank deposit for the grocery store.

Exercise #7: Distillation

Distillation Poem after 3 weeks:

> A rainbowed sunset
> hushed in suspended silence
> the dregs of life's detritus
> of fading glory
> An encroaching ebony pall
> The sinewy cat:
> everyday trivia roused it to animation
> a wide-sweeping emptying
> that covered and coveted
> leaving the body a possession
> and not a vessel.
> When time appears to squander one's body

a wild kaleidoscope of images arise

flora had already dealt her a stinging blow,

the fauna would deal her

even more lethal blows

Distillation Writing after 3 weeks:

I will not give in, not again. Who defines us, who makes us real? The events of our lives mean nothing in the end because they end. Why hasn't someone come back to prove life continues? What does that say for truth?

How does one obtain freedom from the self in which one is currently imprisoned? It's not like one can open the body's door, take a walk to the local Personal Encasement Outlet and choose a new housing unit that fits both budget and aesthetic style. What if bodies were interchangeable? How much influence would a new body have on the inhabiting personality? To be who we are and yet someone else simultaneously — is that not the ultimate in freedom?

It's a miracle, really, that we ever find our way through the maze of life and emerge into the other side, whatever, wherever that might be, relatively unscathed. Though most of us are fairly well scathed even if we won't admit it, scathing being one of the major purposes for life. There is beauty in the loneliness, love in the despair, self-knowledge in the fruit of life. All we need is the courage to pick and eat. And share…

Explore the reality that lies beyond reality, the world of creation, of imagination, of energy and isolation, connectedness and separation. This physical world we walk through exists only in our minds, in the dreams we forget to dream, in the places where we hide from life by living. Beyond all that is truth, the answers questioned and the questions answered. We stand still and travel nowhere and everywhere simultaneously. In that place of nothing and everything, the two halves of our being merge into unity. We know and not know, love and not love, care and not care, hope and not hope. Each second of non-time ticks away with agonizing slowness as it races around the dark wind-swept clock-face of living life. We are more than the flesh and blood that houses us. We are beyond purpose, we have eclipsed meaning. We are end and void and abyss: the trinity of mankind. We are, we simply are, whether in dreams or thought or life or living. Nothing else matters. Nothing else is.

Exercise #8: Voice and Style

First off, on the surface my style is verbose. I love words, and I love exploring what words can evoke in readers. I like to sprinkle unusual words in my narrative, to make the reader really think. I guess that's the first of the techniques I use. I also use very vivid description of both setting and character to pull the reader into the story, to make them feel they know the characters and live in the same places the characters live in. Another technique I use is the cliff-hanger ending to each of my chapters, to nudge the reader to keep reading, and to set up expectation in their minds. And I love to add a number of subplots, just to make it more interesting and convoluted.

My philosophy of life is that there is always a purpose to everything, even if you never know what it is. Nothing happens at random, no matter how random it may feel. We are all connected, all pieces of a greater whole, like drops in the ocean. You can't ever do anything to anyone without it affecting the whole, and especially yourself. Also, you never can know what someone will do or say until it happens. You might think you know someone because you love them or have lived with them for years. But the truth is, we all live isolated in our own heads, and rarely let even ourselves see who we really are, stripped of all pretenses and illusions. We are strangers even to ourselves, searching for meaning, for understanding and belonging.

Which leads me to my theme: in my stories I explore self-discovery. In every story I have at least one character (if not all of them) searching for some kind of identity, some kind of belonging in a world alien to his or her inner life. It's no accident that two of my books have the word Identity in their titles. It probably comes from being adopted at an older age, from not knowing my true parentage and from losing my own identity and having to search for years to rebuild it. My themes revolve around a character discovering who she (or he) is, where she fits into the world, and what her purpose for being is. Because I'm a romantic, these questions are usually answered, or at least partially answered, in a positive way by the end of the story.

To write like me, in my style, would take someone with a good vocabulary who enjoys playing with words, and who has a facility with vivid description. The writer would have to be able to touch his own deep emotions and infuse them into the writing. Like me, this person would have to have experienced isolation, felt like an outsider looking in at a world forever closed to him, and felt cut adrift from life at some point in his own life. He would have to have survived the depths of despair and learned that life is a journey that has no true ending. He would have to have faith in eternity and happy endings, even while doubting the truth of it. He'd have to be a romantic through-and-through, living for the illusion and trusting the illusion is more true than the reality.

Exercise #9: Know Thyself—Style

To be a working writer I need (*and what's stopping me*):

1. A new chair— *money stopping me*
2. Printer for laptop— *have to find disk and set it up and don't know how*
3. Freedom to stay up and write all night— *have to work in the daytime*
4. Financial security— *have to bring in money over SS payments*
5. Less stress— *it's part of life, can't get rid of it*
6. Deadlines— *need to set some of my own*
7. Writing groups— *already belong to too many and want more!*
8. Work editing manuscripts— *have one, need to solicit more*
9. House cleaner— *can't afford it at this point*
10. Cook— *ridiculous to even think about this!*
11. Leisure time for TV, knitting, reading— *I tend to binge on these and waste time on doing it too much*
12. Time to travel— *time and money stopping me*
13. Computer lessons for Facebook, blogging, etc.—*money to pay someone stopping me, and fear I can't understand it*
14. Filing system— *need file cabinet or something*
15. Writing partner to encourage me and push me to finish— *need to find just the right person, though groups help with this for now.*

Priorities: 1, 3, 4, 6, 9 & How to get them.

1. **A new chair:** I can just go spend the money for a new chair to make it more comfortable to sit for long periods at either computer. Sometimes you gotta spend it to make it.
2. **Freedom to write all night:** This will allow me to get back to my natural rhythms where my writing will flow more easily. Can't do it

while I have to work at an outside job. Solution: quit my job and trust that somehow my writing efforts will bring in enough money to survive.

3. **Financial Security:** Will decrease stress and worry, allowing me to concentrate on writing. Inheritance from a writing friend might be enough to supplement for a while, and my son owes me money which he can send each month to help out. Game plan: get my writing books out and hopefully they will generate enough income on their own, then get my suspense books out, too, to augment the income.

4. **House Cleaner:** What's stopping me is the same old/same old—money. But since I live alone I can do with a once-a-month service that maybe I can afford.

5. **Deadlines:** I know myself and I need deadlines to meet to force myself to finish pieces. Hard to make and meet personal deadlines; outside deadline sources work best for me.

Game Plan:

By Thanksgiving:

1. Buy new office chair from Staples.
2. Check out cleaning services and costs/recommendations from friends.
3. Call attorney and see if I can get ballpark figure on inheritance.

By Jan 31, 2012:

1. Quit my job to write/edit full time.
2. Set up payment schedule with son to repay borrowed money.
3. Set up budget for household expenses.

4. Set up a "to-do" list with deadline dates, especially for my own writing that doesn't have specific due dates.

*Author's note: of my Game Plan timeline, all have been accomplished, though I have chosen to to my own cleaning for a while still. I quit my day job so I could concentrate on my writing, editing and teaching.

I have steady (though not a lot) of income coming in from editing work, enough to supplement my social security and ease the financial crunch that was paralyzing me. My son set up a payment schedule on his own before I could approach him with it, which also helps, as do the fees for my classes. My books are now starting to generate some supplemental income, too. The inheritance was enough to supplement about six months.

As of this writing (October, 2014), I have two new novels out in both print and on Kindle and two more scheduled to be released within the next few months along with a book of short pieces. Volume 1 of the *Write It Right Workbooks* is out in print, with volumes 2–4 scheduled out in two weeks. Volumes 5 and 6 should be out by year's end. I have professionally edited books for eight writers and have two others scheduled. I am now on the faculty of the Central Coast Writer's Conference as an editor and panelist, and am looking into presenting a workshop or two at other conferences in the future. (And in between all this I took time out to deal with thyroid cancer and undergo radioactive treatment.)

Knowing what I needed to succeed and having a specific game plan and time line to accomplish it gave me the confidence to believe I could actually do it, and the nudge I needed to get started. Instead of sitting around wishing, I began taking steps to fulfill my dreams of being a notable writer. And the sense of accomplishment as each step was taken gave me ever more confidence to continue taking steps and come even closer to my dream. I still need that new chair, though. Maybe tomorrow...

Afterword

"The original writer is not one who imitates nobody, but one whom nobody can imitate."

~Francois-Rene de Chateaubriand

BEING A WRITER IS a fascinating occupation. By its very nature it forces us to dig deeply into our inner core, face those things that frighten us, are painful or perhaps even disgust us. And then we bring those things into the light of day—on a piece of paper, whether physical or virtual—and transform them into a story that entertains, teaches and/or enlightens whoever reads it. It helps make the world a better place.

The amount of skill needed to do all that successfully is known fully only to those engaged in the practice itself. Readers come in two main groups: those who cannot conceive of what it takes to write a story, much less an entire book; and those who think it's easy to sit down and pound out a story or book in a few days or weeks. But only the brave actually attempt it.

Everything we learn to increase our writing skills helps improve us human beings. We learn how to see, to hear, to contemplate and to understand in ways that most others never do. We learn to find the weaknesses in our heroes and to use them to strengthen their characters. And, in a way, we are also strengthened. We search for the good in our villains and use that to make them human and comprehensible. And in facing our own dark side, we understand more about ourselves and those around us.

In this **Workbook #4**, you have explored two of the essential skills you need to craft compelling, unforgettable stories, whether they are pure fiction or arise from your own life as memoirs. But you need much more than these three areas of expertise before you find your strength as a writer. The other workbooks in the **Write It Right** series will give you exactly what you need to become the best writer you can possibly be, with exercises that can be used over and over again as your skills continue to grow and develop.

Workbook #1 consists of the first three units of the **Write It Right** series: **Character, Setting** and **Story.** These are the first three essential elements of story telling, the foundation blocks, so to speak, for without compelling characters in unforgettable settings acting out amazing stories, there is nothing to write about. Unit #1, *Character*, gives you 9 lessons to help you create amazing characters readers will want to know about. The second unit, *Setting*, consists of 7 lessons and exercises on crafting compelling settings that will draw readers into your story world. And the third unit, *Story*, presents 10 lessons of how to find and assess story ideas that readers will clamor for.

Workbook #2: Point of View (POV) consists of the fourth unit, *Point of View,* which will take you through the murky waters of point of view (POV). In its 15 lessons and exercises you will learn about straight, emotional and classic POV types, and the advantages and disadvantages of each one. You will then experience their variations and understand when to use which POV type to best advantage in your story telling.

Workbook #3: Plot, Dialogue continues your journey along the writer's path with the fifth unit, *Plot,* and its 8 exercises on crafting flawless, intricate plots that sizzle off the page. You'll discover what plot actually is, the importance of a through line, how to analyze ideas for viable plots and where to find plots in the world around you. The sixth unit, *Dialogue,* presents 8 lessons that will show you how to write sparkling dialogue that sounds perfectly natural while still addressing the six necessary ingredients that make dialogue an integral part of the story. You will learn how to write for your audience, make your characters' voices unique, use idioms to infuse verisimilitude, how to tag properly and how to incorporate subtext into what your characters say.

Workbook #5: Conflict/Tension, Subplot offers 9 lessons in the ninth unit, *Conflict/Tension,* that will show you how to create and sustain the tension that keeps readers turning pages through a series of 9 tension-filled exercises. The strategies contained in the tenth unit, *Subplot,* will help you add depth and dimension to your work by weaving fascinating subplots into your main stories. In this workbook, you will also learn the secret to creating an effective and compelling series that satisfies readers as it pulls them through one volume to the next.

Workbook #6: Beginnings, Endings gives you 8 different formats each for opening your story and for ending your story. In the eleventh unit, *Brilliant Beginnings*, you will also learn how to polish that all-important first sentence/first paragraph/first page so that readers are compelled to continue reading. And in the twelfth unit, *Extraordinary Endings*, you will learn the secrets to choosing the proper ending for whatever story you write, so that readers smile and say, "I'm so glad I read that!"

Look for the entire **Write It Right: Exercises to Unlock the Writer in Everyone** workbook series on Amazon.com in print format (each cover is a different color). Each individual unit will eventually also be available in digital format in the Kindle store, but the workbooks themselves are available only in print because I feel that is the most useful format for serious writers. You can have the book open on your desk as you work on the exercises either by hand of on the computer, and not have to keep switching from one window to another to check on the exercise parameters or re-read the lesson as you work.

Thank you for purchasing this Workbook. I hope you find it helpful on your writing journey. If you do, please take the time to write a review on Amazon.com, since that's where most of my sales come from. In this digital age of social media, it's reader reviews that best help sell books. As does word of mouth, so be sure to tell all your writer friends about the Write It Right series, so they can also benefit from the program.

Also, if you'd like, please drop by my website (www.SusanTuttleWrites.com) and leave a comment or two about the photos and story/character/setting ideas you'll find (Category: Woman of 1,000 Words), the weekly writing prompts that post every Wednesday (Category: Write Over The Hump), about the *Write It Right* program, or any other writing subject that comes to mind. Or email me at aim2write@yahoo.com. I'd love to hear from you.

Susan's Books

I NEVER THOUGHT, WHEN I started to write my own stories, that one day I would produce an entire series of workbooks on how to write fiction (and creative nonfiction, because these days that genre needs to be structured in the same manner as fiction). I never thought it even when I started teaching fiction writing. Getting my novels out was my main goal. But life has a way of guiding you down paths you don't even know are there, and this is where I've been led.

What follows is a listing of the books I have out in either print or ebook format, or both—and those in process of being readied for print/e-format. The *Write It Right Workbooks* head the list, but I'm also adding in my fiction titles at the end (suspense and paranormal suspense) in case you might like to take a peek at them, too (all available on Amazon.com and Amazon Kindle). I think they're pretty great, but then, as the author, I'll admit I'm a bit prejudiced.

My hope is that my *Write It Right Workbooks* will help unlock the talent and amazing stories that reside in each and every one of you. Happy writing!

Susan's Nonfiction Books

Write It Right Workbooks available from Amazon Print:

Workbook #1: Units 1, 2, 3: Character, Setting, Story

Workbook #2: Unit 4: POV,

Workbook #3: Units 5, 6: Plot, Dialogue

Workbook #4: Units 7, 8: Scenes, Style/Voice, Conflict

Workbook #5: Units 9, 10: Conflict/Tension, Subplot*

Workbook #6: Units 11, 12: Beginnings, Endings*

Write It Right Individual Units available from Amazon Kindle:

Volume 1: Character

Volume 2: Setting

Volume 3: Story

Volume 4: Point of View (POV)

Volume 5: Plot*

Volume 6: Dialogue*

Volume 7: Scenes*

Volume 8: Style and Voice*

Volume 9: Conflict/Tension*

Volume 10: Subplot*

Volume 11: Brilliant Beginnings*

Volume 12: Extraordinary Endings*

*Coming soon

Susan's Fiction Books

Suspense
> *Tangled Webs*
> *Sins of the Past*

Paranormal Suspense
> *Proof of Identity*

Coming Soon:
> *Piece By Piece*, suspense
> *Obsession*, suspense
> *A Matter of Identity*, historical suspense
> *Stealing Shyon*, and adult fantasy
> The Skylark Series: paranormal detectives
>> *The Somewhen Murder*
>> *Dead Ringer*
>> *Tattooed in Death*
> *Destany's Daughter*, Volume 1 of a paranormal YA/Adult fantasy
>> quadrilogy
> *It Takes Class: On The Short Side*, free writes from my classes